Anonymous

The Fisherman's Children

Or, The Sunbeam of Hardrick Cove. A Tale for the Young.

Anonymous

The Fisherman's Children
Or, The Sunbeam of Hardrick Cove. A Tale for the Young.

ISBN/EAN: 9783744742733

Printed in Europe, USA, Canada, Australia, Japan

Cover: Foto ©Andreas Hilbeck / pixelio.de

More available books at **www.hansebooks.com**

Fisherman's Children;

OR, THE

SUNBEAM OF HARDRICK COVE.

A Tale for the Young.

By the Author of
"HOPE ON," "KING JACK OF HAYLANDS," ETC.

———•———

London:
T. NELSON AND SONS, PATERNOSTER ROW.
EDINBURGH; AND NEW YORK.

1882.

Contents.

" And children too may do God's will,
    Each in his lowly earthly place.

        .   .   .   .   .

Like Him, the lowly child, who dwelt
    Where gleams the Galilean sea,
Whose meat it was to do Thy will—
    Our Guide, our Trust. our Pattern, He."

THE SUNBEAM OF HARDRICK COVE.

CHAPTER I.

THE FISHERMAN'S CHILDREN.

" Briskly blows the evening gale,
   Fresh and free it blows;
Blessings on the fishing-boat,
   How merrily it goes.

" Christ, he loved the fishermen
   Walking by the sea;
How he blessed the fishing-boats
   Down in Galilee ! "

THE baby would *not* go to sleep, though the little girl who held it sung to it gently, and rocked it in her arms as she sat on the step of the cottage door.

It was a fisherman's dwelling, built in a little cove on the sea-shore, and close to the small fishing village of Hardrick, on the coast of Cornwall.

Jacob Williams, its owner, had been a sailor during the early part of his life, but when he was married he gave up his sea-faring life and settled down at Hardrick as a fisherman; and on account of his steady, persevering habits and his former experience, he was looked up to as quite an authority in those parts.

He had three children now, and there was one who was never mentioned, but who was always in his thoughts, who slept in the little churchyard within sound of the breakers on the shore where he had met his death. Jacob had never been the same man since his sailor-boy had been drowned. But still there were some left for him to love. There was his little lame daughter Gracie, whose sweet face and gentle ways were a perpetual delight to him, and whose infirmity made her only more dear to his loving, fatherly heart; there was music to his ear in the sound of her crutch, in her ringing laugh, and low, clear voice; and often and often when at his employment, during long days and stormy nights, his mind was cheered with the thought of the smile that would light up her face, and the cry of joy that would break from her, when she heard "father's step" upon the shingle. And then there was "mother's pet," as he was always called,— the merry, laughing, mischievous Frank, who would get his way in everything, and who was the most active, playful, and handsome boy that lived in Hardrick.

Frank Williams was a general favourite, and was welcome everywhere; the fishermen unloading their boats smiled at the tricks of the boy as he pretended to help them, told him a hundred times to keep out of the way, and yet missed him if he was not in the harbour when they came in. The mothers who were busy in their cottages nodded to Frank as he passed, and gladly trusted their wee toddling things to his charge to be taken on the shore, knowing that, wild as he was, he would be faithful to his trust; and the children looked up in his face with perfect faith, feeling quite secure of his kindness and gentleness, and believing that he would always defend them from the roughness and teasing of the village torment, Ralph Lennox.

Gracie was not, to the eye of the casual observer, so calculated to win affection as her merry brother; and she seemed to know this herself, for there was a timid shrinking in her manner, and she was accustomed always to give place to Frank, thinking that it would be quite wrong if people did not admire and love him as much as she did herself. But yet there were some who loved Gracie more than Frank. There was an old fisherman at the other side of the harbour, whom Gracie always called Uncle Peter, and who always called her "Sunshine," and watched for her daily visit as the chief brightness of his lonely life.

There was old Dame Kenrick, who could'

not see to read the blessed Book, but who knew that Gracie would never pass her door without going in to brighten her up by reading some of those words of comfort which she could think of for the rest of the day ; and her little grandson Abel, who had been ill for such a long time, while his face got paler and thinner, and his childish strength dwined

ABEL.

away, had watched for the sound of Gracie's crutch, and welcomed her approach to the cottage door, where his father placed his small wooden chair every morning when the sun shone. But Abel had gone to heaven now, and David, his father, had grown reckless, people said, since his little white-faced boy had died, and changed his honest occupation of fishing for some work of dishonesty, and had given up the little cottage by the sea; and now nobody knew where he lived, though he was sometimes seen, in the gloom of the evening, stealing along the shore. Some said he was a wrecker, and watched with greedy eyes for the spoils washed up by the waves; and some called him Kenrick the sheep-stealer; but he was the village mystery, and when mothers wanted to frighten their children into good behaviour, they threatened them with the name of "wicked Kenrick."

But we have wandered a long way from the cottage door, where we left Gracie singing the baby to sleep. It took a long time, for the baby was not inclined to do as its sister wished; and Gracie with wistful eyes

watched the red sun going down over the
sea, and knew that Uncle Peter was watching for her, and that Frank was down in
the fishing harbour seeing the nets dragged
in, and father's boat would be coming in
soon, and she would not be down on the
shore to meet him ; and it required all her
patience not to shake the baby by way of
hastening its slumbers.

"Gracie, Gracie," cried a merry voice at
her side, " Uncle Peter says you must come
down to the harbour. Father's boat is coming
in, and they've got a haul of mackerel—none
of your common pilchard this time, but
beautiful coloured mackerel—and they're
leaping up in the net. Come quick, Gracie."

" I can't, Frank, I can't. Look, baby's wide
awake, and she'll cry if I put her down."

" Mother will mind her till you come back;
I'll ask her,"—and there was a touch of
superiority in the boy's tone, as if he knew
that *he* could be refused nothing, though
Gracie might. A little sigh burst from

Gracie as she heard the emphasis he laid upon the words "I'll ask her;" but it was quickly stopped, for she had learned to "esteem others better than herself;" and quietly checking Frank's impetuosity by laying her disengaged hand on his arm, she said, "Don't, Frank; mother's busy; she don't want baby now. I'd rather stop, please."

"Well, you're a fool to lose such a chance, that's all; but good-bye, I'm off!"

And still Gracie sat on with the restless baby. For a moment or two a cloud overshadowed the sweet calm of her face, but it passed away as she gazed out towards the sunset, and watched the sun slowly dipping down behind the water, and casting a bright red glow over the harbour, the fishing-boats, and the sturdy fishermen who were drawing in their nets. She was not near enough to distinguish faces, but she knew that her father's voice was amongst those which she heard mingling with the noise of the waves; and when she looked down into her little sister's face she saw that she was asleep, so, quietly rising up, she went into the cottage, where her mother was ironing some blue shirts of her father's, and laying her finger on her lips, said in a hushed voice, " Mother, she's fast asleep ; " then gently laying little Peggy in the cradle, she added, "May I go down to the beach now, mother ? "

Her mother was hot and irritated by her work, which she had not got through as quickly as she wished, and she looked round the disorderly room, and replied curtly, " You're always running off to that beach; you should have a thought now and then that there's work to be done at home. What's the use of you setting up to be better than your neighbours, if you don't practise it?"

Gracie coloured. " I haven't been down in the harbour all day, mother."

" Well, and what business has a big girl like you always to be running after the fishermen ? "

" Frank goes," replied Gracie.

"Frank's a boy," said her mother, taking an iron from the fire, energetically rubbing it on the blanket, and then holding it to her cheek, while Gracie stood twirling her bonnet on one finger and looking out of the window. There was a long silence, and at last the little girl said, "Mayn't I go, then?"

"Oh, go off if you like," said her mother angrily. So Gracie went.

But she was not happy; she did not look at the scene in the harbour with the same pleasure she had done a few minutes before; she did not feel as if she had done right; and there darted into her mind the words which were her daily motto, "If any man will come after me, let him deny himself and take up his cross and follow me." She was trying to come after her Master, and surely for his sake she should take up this little cross; and so she turned round and entered the cottage, saying brightly, "Please, mother, I would rather help you."

Her mother smiled; she did not know the

motive which influenced her little daughter,
but she guessed that it was some of "Gracie's
queer notions," which she was quite content
that she should keep so long as they made
her the useful and sweet-tempered child
that she was at home, though she could
never be like her pet Frank. And Gracie
folded up the clothes that were scattered
over the table, and put some coal on the
fire, filled the kettle and set it on, brushed
up the hearth, put the net which Frank was
making into the corner, and then turned
round with a smile to ask her mother if there
was anything else which she could do. The
ironing was finished, and Dame Williams
was folding up the blanket, and putting the
pile of clothes into her husband's sea-chest,
which was the receptacle for all the family
wearing apparel. Now that the work was
over, the good woman was relieved, and
both herself and her temper began gradually
to cool down, and she looked kindly at her
daughter and said,—

"No, thank ye, my dear—you're growing a nice handy little maid. I wonder father isn't come in."

"They had a haul of mackerel, mother," said Gracie, her heart beating fast with pleasure at the unusual praise bestowed upon her, and feeling at that moment as if no mackerel haul she had ever seen was as well worth looking at as that kind smile on mother's face.

"Mackerel was it, child?   Are you sure it was mackerel?"

"Yes, mother; Frank came up and told me."

"Why didn't you go to see them? it's a pretty sight, a mackerel haul."

"Baby wasn't asleep then," said Gracie looking down, so that she did not see her mother's approving glance ; but Dame Williams was quick of comprehension, she knew directly the sacrifice which the child had made, and as she walked over to the cupboard to get out the tea-things she stroked

Gracie's hair back from her forehead, and stooping down, left a hearty kiss there. This was no common thing, and Gracie put it away in her mind to be thought of in quiet corners and at happy times, and always to bring a thrill of joy to the heart of the loving child.

And now there was a shout at the cottage door, and Frank burst in with a fine mackerel dangling by its tail.

"There, mother,—there, Gracie,—that's mine. I dodged down under Uncle Peter's arms, and I dragged this one out of the net; and they called me thief—and I laughed, and told them it would be so good for my supper; and father's got beauties—a fine haul —here he comes." And just as Gracie reached the door her father met her.

"Well, Mother Carey, why didn't you come when I sent for you?" ("Mother Carey's Chicken" was the pet name which he had given to his little daughter, in re-membrance of his early days, and the birds which he had so often protected in a storm, when they had sought refuge in the ship to which he belonged.)

"I was busy, father; I couldn't come then."

THE FATHER'S RETURN.

"Silly lass, it's not every day we have such a haul—no pilchard this time. Uncle Peter was lost without you; so I promised you should go over to-morrow night and make his cup o' tea, and show him you know how to broil a fish."

A great hug was Gracie's only answer; and then she turned to admire Frank's mackerel, and to help her mother in getting the evening meal ready for the hungry fisherman.

CHAPTER II.

TEA WITH UNCLE PETER.

" The roseate hues of early dawn,
    The brightness of the day,
    The crimson of the sunset sky,—
    How fast they fade away !

" Oh ! for the pearly gates of heaven,
    Oh ! for the golden floor,
    Oh ! for the Sun of Righteousness
    That setteth nevermore ! "

"ERE I am, Uncle Peter—here I am," said Gracie merrily, as she stood in the doorway of his hut the next evening, a little before sundown.

There was no mistaking it for anything but a fisherman's abode, for outside the door there was the half of a boat standing on end, with a seat inside it, where Uncle

Peter used to smoke his pipe, and which
Gracie called his summer-house; on the
rocks near the cottage some nets were
spread, and two oars were lying about; but
the interior of the dwelling was as tidy as
possible, though its furniture was scant and
poor. However, Uncle Peter always said it
was enough for him, and he would not have
exchanged it for the finest in the world.

" Why, Sunbeam, I began to think you
wasn't coming any more, that you'd got
tired of the old man and his yarns."

" Then you are a very bad old uncle, and
I'll go away again if you say that."

" No, you won't," said the old fisherman,
putting his arm round her, and kissing her.
" Now, what have you been doing with yourself ? "

" Mother wanted me."

" Why, I thought you told me that no
one ever wanted you except me."

" Well, but, Uncle Peter, don't you know
you told me something then about trying to

be useful, and I have been trying, and so now people do want me."

"That's right, my lass; and so you're learning that though you mayn't be able to be a little craft yourself, you can still be an oar to help other crafts on."

"Yes, Uncle Peter," replied the child, smiling at his simile.

"No, no, lass, our great Captain, he won't have none of his hands idle; from the chief mate down to the lad that mops the deck, every one's got their own work, and they must see to do it, that it's done," continued the old man thoughtfully.

It was to Uncle Peter that Gracie owed her "queer notions;" partly, at least. He had strengthened the early impressions which her brother George had made ; for long ago the young sailor had told her "that sweet story of old," of the holy life and death of the Saviour of mankind, ·and prayed that his little sister might be brought into the fold of the Good Shepherd and made one of his lambs; and now his prayer was being answered, and Gracie was being led into the "green pastures" and "beside the still waters" which he had found so peaceful; and in her life the fruits of the Holy Spirit were becoming daily more and more visible.

"Uncle Peter, do you know, there's one bad thing about coming to you, and only one," said the little girl as she hung her bonnet up.

"What's that, dearie?"

"Why, I hate passing Simon Lennox's cottage, for if Ralph's outside he's sure to call out, 'Humpty Dumpty,' or 'Run it, cripple,' or something cruel; and sometimes he comes out and stops me—to-night he did."

"And what did *you* do?"

"I looked him straight in the face and said, 'I'm not afraid of you, Ralph Lennox.'"

"He's a shocking bad lad," said Peter.

"Indeed he is; father doesn't like Frank going with him, but he does sometimes."

"He's got a dreadful home, poor chap;

his father drinks—his mother's dead—and
his aunt scolds him terribly. I've seen the
lad turned out of doors late on a winter's
night, and allowed to stop out all night;
and then I've had him in here, and let him
warm himself, and given him a bit of my
mind; but he has generally made a face at
me, and gone off with an oath. Oh, he'll
come to some bad end!"

"I hope not," said little Gracie, putting
her hands over her eyes; and in her heart
there rose up a deep and strong yearning for
the wretched, loveless boy—poor, poor Ralph.

"Now, Gracie, we'll have our tea; and
then we'll go down to the Point, and I'll
take you out in the *Sea Gull* for a bit."

Gracie's eyes brightened with delight, she
did so enjoy an evening with Uncle Peter;
and then she moved about quietly arranging
their little meal, and broiled some fish in
her best style; while the old man sat at his
door and smoked.

When tea was over, Uncle Peter took

down an old pea-jacket, and made Gracie
put it on, to keep her "tight and warm," as
he said. She looked a funny little figure
with her cottage bonnet, her golden curls
peeping out underneath it, her pale face lit
up by a sunshiny smile of pleasure, her
simple little dress of dark blue, and the big
jacket over all coming down to her heels.
Uncle Peter laughed heartily when he
looked at her, and then took her hand, and
they set off in the direction of the Point,
where his little white rowing-boat lay
moored. Very gently the old man helped
the little girl over the wet and slippery
rocks, into a comfortable seat in the stern,
where she sat to steer, and then taking up
his oars, he began to push off from the
shore; and Gracie in silent delight sat
listening to the splash of the oars, and
watching them dip into the clear water, so
smoothly and steadily that it seemed no
trouble or exertion for the boat to go so fast.

"Look, Uncle Peter! Oh, do you see

the sun's glory path ? " she cried at length,
as she pointed to the glowing track of light
which was thrown across the sea from the
setting sun.

The old man smiled, and turned the boat
in that direction, fixing his eyes on the
glorious scene as though it possessed some
fascination for him.

" What is it like, Uncle Peter ? " said the
little girl thoughtfully.

" Like many things, my child ; the sunset
is a sermon to me every day."

Gracie still looked inquiringly, for she
loved the simple fancies of the old fisherman, and he went on,—

" It's like the Christian's path to heaven.
Christ the beginning of the way, Christ the
whole of the way, and Christ himself—the
Sun of Righteousness—in fuller glory at the
end of the way."

Gracie looked up full of pleasure. " O
Uncle Peter, I think it's like the hymn we
had last Sunday,—

" ' A light to shine upon the road
That leads me to the Lamb.' "

" Yes, you're right, Sunbeam; and do you see how the path gets brighter as it gets nearer the sun ?—' the path of the just is as the shining light, which shineth more and more unto the perfect day '—the perfect day; O Gracie, child, what a day that'll be, with no squalls, no clouds, nothing but clear sunshine."

" Don't you think King Solomon must have been looking at the sunset when he wrote that ? "

" Yes, child," said the old fisherman ; but his eyes were fixed on the sinking sun, and the " glory path," as if his thoughts were away at the end of the pathway where all his hopes and affections were fixed, and he continued, as if speaking to himself, " Yes, the waters of this stormy sea of life may be rough and raging all round, but what need the Christian mind so long as that light shines across them and leads him to his home ? ' Walk as children of light,' " he added aloud.

And Gracie repeated the words to herself, as her eyes wandered in the direction of the cottage home upon the shore where her life-work was carried on.

" Sing to me, Gracie," said Peter at length, after he had rowed on for some time in silence.

Gracie thought for a moment, and then began in a sweet, clear voice, which sounded peculiarly so as the little boat glided through the water, the hymn commencing—

" Why those fears ?   Behold, 'tis Jesus
Holds the helm and guides the ship."

It was a long one, and the little girl did not sing all the verses, but chose out those which she knew Uncle Peter loved best ; and the old man's voice chimed in with the child's, as she sang,—

" Though the shore we hope to land on
Only by report is known,
Yet we freely all abandon,
Led by that report alone,
And with Jesus
Through the trackless deep move on.

"Rendered safe by his protection,
 We shall pass the watery waste;
Trusting to his wise direction,
 We shall gain the port at last,
  And with wonder
Think on toils and dangers past."

"Ay, ay," said Uncle Peter. "Thank you, lass; I often think of that when I'm out in my fishing-smack. There's the last of the sun, child, and it will be getting cold on the water."

"And mother said I mustn't be late going home," said Gracie.

So Uncle Peter turned the boat round, and began rowing in towards the shore.

"Button that jacket up round your throat, Gracie."

She did so, nestling her head down into the warmth of the collar.

"Are you warm, dearie?"

"Yes, Uncle Peter. Oh, I'm so happy— I do love you so much!"

"Thank you, little Sunshine; it b'aint many that's left to love old Peter *now;*" and there was a mournful tenderness in his voice as he said the last words, and yet he added in an undertone, as if to comfort himself, "*I* have loved thee with an everlasting love."

No more words were exchanged until they reached the Point, where Uncle Peter moored the boat in safety, and gently lifted Gracie out of it, carrying her over the rocks until they reached the smooth sand, where he put her down and took her hand as they walked up to his cottage.

"Now, Uncle Peter, I must be going," said Gracie.

"I'll take you back along the shore," said Uncle Peter, when he had put his oars away in safety behind the house.

"No. no, Uncle Peter; please, I would rather not," said Gracie earnestly, for a desire had sprung up in her heart, which she hoped to put into execution; besides which she knew that Uncle Peter was getting old and infirm, and had had a hard day's labour.

"But aren't you afraid of passing Simon Lennox's cottage ?"

"No, not now—indeed, I'm not. I would rather, Uncle Peter. There, now, let me light your pipe and be off."

The old man consented, and sitting down under the shadow of the boat, waited until Gracie came out with his lit pipe, and

THE GOOD-NIGHT.

divested of his pea-jacket, for which she had exchanged her own little brown cape.

"Good-night, Uncle Peter; I've had a fine time to-night."

"So have I, dearie; may the Almighty bless thee, and bring thee safe to port at last," he added tenderly, as he kissed her forehead; and then he watched her fondly, as, leaning on her crutch, she made slow progress along the shore, until a turn in the rocks hid her from his sight, and he relapsed into deep thought.

His was a simple, trusting mind. He had not escaped the buffeting of "the waves of this troublesome world," but the heavenly Pilot was his friend, and he was—

"Calm amidst tumultuous motion,
Knowing that his Lord was nigh."

His wife had died when he was comparatively young, leaving him two children. His boy Jack, who had been his greatest pride, had been drowned at sea before his eyes; and his daughter Mary, weary of the quiet life on the shore, and hearing grand stories of the pleasures and delights of town, had run away from her home, and never been heard of since, though every night Uncle Peter took a long look up and down the shore in the hope of seeing the wanderer returning; but night after night, and year after year passed away, and still she came not; and her name was nearly forgotten at Hardrick, except in that loving father's heart, who prayed daily that God would bring back his stray lamb, as he fondly called her. And in calm and steadfast trust, the old man looked out over the sea, and thought lovingly and rejoicingly of those who had gone before him, and whose barks were safely moored "in the haven where they would be."

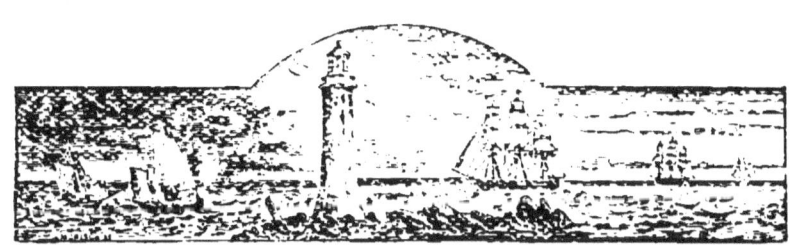

CHAPTER III.

GRACIE'S MINISTRY OF LOVE.

"So deeds of love will cheer and bless
A low laborious life ;
So words of peace and gentleness
Glide in and soften strife."

LITTLE Gracie, meanwhile, was walking home very thoughtfully and slowly, though her heart began to beat faster as she came in sight of Simon Lennox's cottage, and she feared that either the drunken sailor himself or his scolding sister might appear ; so she quickened her steps a little, and, as she neared the wretched abode, she saw the door opened, and Ralph forcibly pushed outside it. He turned round crying with rage and passion, and Gracie heard some wicked words fall from his lips; and then, sitting down upon a rock near the cottage door, the boy cried bitterly; in fact, it was hardly a cry that he uttered, but rather a howl of rage and fury mixed with pain, for he was smarting from his aunt's blows.

Gracie's courage melted away, and she tried to pass him as quickly as she could, hoping that he would not see her; but as she did so her thoughts wandered back to Uncle Peter's teaching, and she remembered reading the parable of the Good Samaritan to him one day; and now she felt that she was behaving just like the Levite and the priest, whose conduct she had then condemned so severely, for she too was "passing by on the other side" when a fellow-creature was in trouble and distress. Surely she could return good for evil now; and so she went up to Ralph, and said, in a low, gentle voice, "Poor Ralph!"

The boy started. Who could have spoken? Surely no one could be saying that to *him*—

" Poor Ralph!"—and the voice which said the words so gentle and so soft.   He raised his head, and his eyes fell upon Gracie.

His was a strange face ; there was such a wonderful mixture in it.   There were the dark eyes, black hair, and olive complexion that belong to most of the children in that part of England ; but the eyes had a wild, cunning, and yet frightened expression in them, the mouth had a sullen compression, and the cheeks were haggard and pale.   He looked like a half-starved creature, and the blood which streamed from his nose in consequence of one of the blows he had received increased his wretched appearance.   And yet, miserable and revolting as he looked, Gracie softly repeated the words, " Poor Ralph ! "

He held his hand up to stop the flow of blood, but only muttered,—

" Go along; I don't want none of your talk;" and yet there was a strange feeling in his heart, produced by those simple words of the child whom he had delighted to tease by his cruel remarks, a feeling as if he longed to hear her say them again.

" I'm so sorry for you," said Gracie simply; " your nose is bleeding—are you hurt much?"

" Yes," and an oath followed; but Gracie saw that he was becoming whiter and whiter, and feared that he was going to faint.

" Put your head back upon that rock— there, that way—and I'll get some water for you," said the little girl quickly; and, looking about, she spied one of those old tin cans which continually are seen lying in the vicinity of a cottage, bent, dinged, and battered, and generally with a hole in the bottom, which prevents them any longer from filling the post of conveying "father's dinner" to him. Gracie picked up one of this kind, dropped a quantity of sea-weed into the bottom of it, and then dipped it into one of the clear pools of sea-water amongst the rocks, after which she took out of her pocket her own little check handkerchief, and, soaking it in the water, held it to poor Ralph's nose. The feeling

THE GOOD SAMARITAN.

of the cold water against his face soon revived him, and when he no longer saw the blood streaming over his hand, the sight of which had turned him sick and faint before, he grew better and raised himself up a little. But then the thought of his injuries came back to him, and he howled louder than ever.

"Don't, don't, Ralph, please don't," cried Gracie; "I can't bear to hear you cry. What's the matter?"

" Why they've turned—they've turned
me out ! "

" Who ? " asked Gracie, wondering if she
could help or comfort him in any way.

" Aunt Poll; she knocked me over the
head 'cos I hadn't done nothing."

" Well, go in now," suggested his little
comforter.

" She'd thrash me again, or make dad do
it."

" What had you done ? "

" I hadn't done nothing, only upset the
pot that was boiling."

" That *was* something, Ralph."

" She's always a-beating and thrashing
me, and I'd like to give it her, I should—
ooh !—ooh !—ooh ! " and a prolonged howl
followed the words.

" Hush, Ralph; please don't," said Gracie;
but Ralph found it a relief to vent his angry
feelings in words, and went on,—

" I wish I was a man, growed up, I'd get
the toughest broomstick I could find, and

I'd thrash Aunt Poll all day; and every time she cried out, I'd lay it on harder."

"O Ralph, don't say such wicked, dreadful words."

"I would, I tell you, I would—I'd thrash her till she couldn't stand."

"Then you would be a coward," said Gracie bravely; "for my father says none but a coward would raise his hand to a woman."

"I wouldn't raise my hand, I'd raise the broomstick, because it would lay on harder," said Ralph, whose sobs were subsiding as the pain gradually went off.

"The rain is coming on; won't you go and ask her to let you come in? It's clouding over, and Uncle Peter said he thought it would be a wet night."

"She wouldn't let me in, I tell you."

"But you'll get wet."

"It wouldn't be the first time," he replied sullenly, as he rose up to look at the black clouds which were gathering overhead; but he staggered back again, dizzy and weak. " I can't stand."

"What is the matter ? "

" She beat me with the back of a brush ; and I've had nothing to eat to-day."

" Poor Ralph," said the pitying little Gracie softly ; and then added, with a great effort, " I'll go and ask her to let you in, and you can go to bed."

"Do !" said Ralph earnestly ; and so Gracie summoned up all her courage and went to the cottage door. Her first knock was so feeble that it was not heard, but her second was louder, and Ralph's aunt lifted the latch.

Poll Lennox was a tall, powerful woman ; she had a rough, hard, weather-beaten face, with a most repulsive scowl upon it, and she spoke like a man, walked like a man, and, had it not been for her striped woollen petticoat, looked like a man ; for, in addition to this, she wore a glazed hat constantly, a blue pea-jacket with brass buttons, and men's boots. The sleeves of the jacket were now rolled up, and revealed a pair of red and brawny arms. Gracie trembled as this fierce-looking woman addressed her in an angry voice,—

"What do you want?"

"I want Ralph's Aunt Poll."

"Well?"

"I want for Ralph to come in;" but her voice trembled at the end of the sentence, and her eyes filled with tears.

"What business is it of yours, girl? Go off with yourself."

"Please let him in; it's going to rain."

"A wetting may take some of the sauce out of him."

"But please let him in, he's sick and dizzy."

"Will you go along, or must I make you?" said Poll with a meaning gesture.

"I'm going, but I'm afraid Ralph will get sick if he's out in the wet, and he's so white, and his nose has been bleeding badly."

"*Will* you be off?" said Poll, slamming the door in her face; and Gracie, baffled and disappointed, returned to where Ralph was sitting awaiting her arrival.

"She won't let you in. I'm so sorry, poor Ralph; and I must go on, or mother will be vexed."

"Go on," said Ralph sulkily. "I knew she wouldn't."

Gracie looked at him for a moment, thinking if there was anything else she could say. There was much she longed to say, but which shyness kept back. And so, after a long, kind, pitying gaze into his miserable face, she said again, "Poor Ralph!" and he saw that tears were running down her cheeks. She quickly raised her hand to wipe them away, and then walked on, very sorrowfully, comparing in her mind Ralph's lot and her own, which she had sometimes thought so hard. Before she turned the corner which shut out Simon Lennox's cottage from her view, she turned round, and had the satisfac-

tion of seeing the cottage door opened, and
Poll's head put out, and of hearing her cry,
"Come in, you young dog, and behave
yourself;" and then she saw poor Ralph rise
up and totter forwards, holding on by the
cottage wall, until the door was shut upon
him, and, with a thankful heart, she continued her walk. The evening shadows
were gathering quickly, and twilight was
fast giving place to darkness; but Gracie
was now within sight of her father's cottage,
and had not much further to go. Neverthe-
less she was destined to meet with another
adventure before reaching home, for she had
not gone very far along the lonely shore,
before she saw a dark figure coming up
towards her, whom, from his ragged appearance and fierce look, she knew to be Kenrick
the sheep-stealer. He never ventured out
except at night, and Gracie had the same
fear of him as all the other village children
possessed, and she walked out nearer to the
sea to avoid him; but Kenrick did not intend

that she should do this, and advanced to meet her. " Good evening, Grace," he said ; and Gracie replied, in a very low voice, " Good evening."

" Look here, I've been watching this many evenings for you."

Gracie got more frightened. What could he mean ? what was he going to do ?

" Please, I'm in a hurry," she said quickly. " I'm out too late. Mother'll be vexed."

" Wait a bit."

" I mustn't wait," said Gracie again, and wishing in her heart that Uncle Peter had been with her.

" Are *you* afraid of me, like the rest of 'em?" said Kenrick, and there was a sorrowful tone in his voice.

Gracie look up into his face wistfully, but there seemed to be something there that satisfied her, for she answered quietly,—

" No, I don't think I'm afraid of you."

" Look here, I've been wanting to give you this; " and he put into her hand an old-

fashioned ornament, with a precious stone
in the middle of it, which flashed and
glittered even in the dim evening light.

"Oh, is it for me?" asked Gracie, her
eyes beaming with pleasure. "Where did
you get this pretty thing?"

"From the sea," replied Kenrick, a strange
smile passing over his face as he spoke.
"You keep it, little one, for Abel's sake."

"Dear little Abel," murmured Gracie.

"Ay, you loved him, and so did I; but it
doesn't matter now, only don't *you* think so
hard of Abel's father as the neighbours do
—d'ye hear?"

"No, I won't," said Gracie; "but—but—"
and she hesitated and coloured very much.

"But what, lass? speak up."

"You aren't what they say you are, are
you?"

"Never mind what they say I am; you
just remember that I'd do anything for you.
And now good-night, and don't be feared of
me when next I meet you."

In an instant he was gone. And then Gracie looked at the pretty jewel in her hand, and wondered where it came from. That had been an adventurous evening, but she was not sorry that she had nearly reached home; and then she saw her father coming to meet her, for he had been smoking his pipe outside the cottage door, and watching for his little daughter's approach.

"Who were you speaking to?" he asked, as soon as he had got up to her.

"David Kenrick, father; and look what he gave me!"

"Phew! how came he to speak to you, child?"

"He wanted to give me this; look, father, this glittering, pretty thing; he says he got it out of the sea!"

"Ay, I'll warrant he did," said Jacob. "Off the body of some poor drowned or drowning creature," he added in a lower tone.

"O father," said little Gracie with a shudder, "is it bad to keep it?"

"No, no, my child; keep it if you fancy it. That's a queer chap."

Gracie *did* fancy it, and so it was laid up with her other little treasures, after having been displayed to all the members of the family, and being commented on rather severely by Dame Williams.

Ralph, meanwhile, had crept away to his little garret-room, and stretched himself, stiff and weary, on his wretched bed. But still there rang in his ears the words spoken by that childish, pitying voice, "Poor Ralph!" and the angry demon within his heart seemed to be silenced by the remembrance.

CHAPTER IV.

A SEA-SIDE TALK.

" There is freedom in the ocean,
　　There is spirit in the breeze,
　　There is life in every motion
　　Of the ever-restless seas.

" With the binding crest of foam
　　In the sunny radiance glancing,
　　And the rippling sounds that come,
　　Still dying, still advancing."

T was a fine clear day, about a week after Gracie's evening with Uncle Peter, and she and Frank were perched on the end of a ledge of rocks which jutted out into the sea at low-water.

"Look, Gracie, there it comes ! I've counted eight ; this is the ninth wave—yes, it *is* a big one—bang ! what a roar it makes ! "

"Father says it's the death-wave," replied Gracie, looking wistfully at the long line of foam breaking along the sandy shore.

"Why?" asked her brother, as he dipped his hand into the pool of sea-water by his side, and played with the bright sea-weeds at the bottom of it.

"Because, sometimes when there's a wreck, the poor sailors have got quite close to shore, and then this big wave comes and dashes them back again."

"Father's boat is out ever so far; look, Gracie, all over there!" and Frank pointed eagerly to a dark speck out on the dancing water. "Oh, I wish I might go in it with him! I shall, when I am bigger."

Gracie looked up fondly into his bright face, and said, "O Frank! George went out, and he never, never came back again. I don't want you to go too!"

"Nonsense, Gracie; that's because you're only a silly girl; you don't suppose every fisherman must be drowned, do you?"

"No, no," replied Gracie gently; "of course I don't, Frank; but it's only that—that—"

"Well, what?" asked her brother impatiently, flinging a stone from the rock on which they were sitting down into the water, which was tumbling and breaking in foam beneath them.

FRANK AND GRACIE.

Gracie laid her little hand quietly on her brother's dark, curly hair, and answered,—

"It's only, Frank, that I don't think I could bear it if anything were to happen to you. George loved me so, and he used to carry me in his arms, and bring me shells, and sea-weeds, and all manner of wonderful things, and lift me up on the high rocks and keep me safe there with his arms round me, while the great waves rolled up against the rock and broke; and then how we used to laugh when the foam dashed up into our faces: and then, one night George went out fishing (not in father's boat, in another), and he never came back. There was a storm, and the boat was upset; he struggled to-wards the shore—he could swim!—and he had nearly reached it, when, oh!" and Gracie covered her face with her hands as if to shut out the sight—"you know it all, Frank—don't you?"

"I never heard it rightly; father never speaks about it, nor mother, and I only remember a noise when I was in bed, and it woke me in my sleep. And then I saw

George next day lying on his bed, and they told me he was dead; but I thought he was asleep, only he looked so white, and his hair all wet with sea-water; but you were down on the beach, Gracie, weren't you?"

"Yes, yes," said Gracie, shuddering; "mother and I. It was moonlight, and we saw him so near the shore; and then a big wave came and washed him away back again. We did not see him for some minutes, and then suddenly another great wave dashed him on shore;—but he was dead. The fishermen and sailors carried him up to the cottage; but oh, Frank, nothing could bring him back—*nothing!*" and the little girl's voice died away mournfully as she repeated the word. There was silence between the brother and sister for some minutes; Gracie was gazing far away to the horizon where the clouds and water seemed to meet, and Frank looked at her thoughtful face, with its deep, earnest eyes, its pale cheeks, and its sweet, calm mouth, and then his eyes wandered down to the crutch which lay beside her.   At last he spoke,—

"Gracie, was George like me, anything?"

"You should rather say, are you like him?" she replied, turning round with a smile.   "I think you will be, Frank; but you know our George was sixteen, and you are only nine."

"I shall be ten, mother says, in seven months more.

"Yes; but you are only nine now."

"Then you are only thirteen."

"I know that; I shall not be fourteen till next month," said Gracie, smiling; "but your hair is dark, and George's was bright and sunny; and your eyes are brown, and his were blue.   I think you *are* like him in other things—you have the same sunburnt face, and rosy cheeks, and smile like him."

"That's why father sighs so sometimes when he looks at me."

"Yes," replied Gracie; "it's five years, Frank, since that dreadful eveniug."

"But look, look, Gracie! the tide is rising; we must get back towards home," and Frank sprang to his feet, and then helped his sister to get up, kindly and gently.

"Let us go into my cove," said Gracie, as she moved with difficulty along the ledge of rock.

Gracie's cove was a little sheltered corner among the rocks where the waves never came; they were stopped by two large boulders at the entrance of this little nook, and expending all their fury in dashing against them with a great roar, they came in gently in small ripples, and broke on the shining sand before they had reached Gracie's seat. This was a kind of natural arm-chair of rock which George had found for her, and another large rock served for a table, while two or three ledges were used for shelves. Here the little girl spent a good part of her life; for, as she was not able

to join in the active sports of the other
children who lived in the small fishing-village
at Hardrick Cove, it was a great pleasure
to her to sit in her little rock-chamber
watching the waves, which seemed like
familiar friends and playmates to her, and
doing some work, or reading in her little
books.

Frank's great delight was to ornament
this little cove for his sister : the wild rock-
creepers and all the flowering plants which
grew near the sea hung in festoons from the
top of it, and were planted around the spot ;
a little mat of plaited sea-weed was under
Gracie's seat ; large shells and stones were
its ornaments, and were arranged with great
taste ; while near the entrance there was a
small natural basin amongst the rocks which
the tide filled each day, and which was full
of beautiful sea-weeds of various colours,
amongst which Frank sometimes discovered
little crabs crawling about to investigate the
premises.

This was Gracie's cove, and she loved it. She and Frank had not long established themselves in it that evening before they spied a face peeping at them from round the corner of the rock.

"There's Ralph!" said Frank, jumping up; and Gracie said merrily,—

"Come in, Ralph; this is my rock-room."

Ralph advanced shyly, and holding out something in his hand, he mumbled,—

"I've come; I've brought it—there's some things for you in it."

"What is it, Ralph?"

"Your rag, you lent me;" and in the discoloured thing he held out, Gracie recognized her little handkerchief. She took it with a smile, and began to untie the various hard knots in which Ralph had fastened up its contents.

"What can it be?" said Gracie; but when the last knot was undone she discovered several sea-gulls' eggs, and one or two light-coloured shells. Frank instantly seized upon the eggs, and Gracie looked up into Ralph's face with a pleased laugh, and said, "I like them very much, Ralph; thank you."

"Where did you get these, Ralph?" cried Frank eagerly; "they're beauties!"

"Ah, I knows where they come from!" said Ralph, grinning with satisfaction at the reception his gift was meeting with.

"Tell us where," said Frank.

"That's a secret," replied Ralph.

"I want to get some."

"It's out there," said Ralph, nodding in the direction of a point of rock in the distance, which was of a peculiarly dark colour, and was generally known by the name of Sea-Gull Point.

Frank's face fell. "I'm not let go there," he said sorrowfully.

Ralph looked at him in surprise.

"Not let! why not? who won't let it?"

"My father."

"And do you really mean that you mind what your dad says?"

"Fathers are made to be obeyed," said Gracie, quoting one of her mother's favourite axioms.

"*I* think dads are meant to be cheated," said Ralph, laughing bitterly. "Anyways, mine is."

"Oh, don't, don't, Ralph,—you mustn't speak like that to us; we love ours, and like to do what he tells us," said Gracie earnestly; but Frank did not speak, for his eyes were fixed longingly on the Point. His father said it was dangerous there because of the way the tide came up, and the shelving of the rocks; but Frank's spirit of adventure was only the more roused by the thought of the danger.

"I'll put your eggs here, amongst my pretty things," said Gracie, arranging them on one of the ledges. "O Ralph, I'll show you something that was given me;" and taking from the bosom of her frock a baby's stocking, she pulled out of it the ornament with the jewel in its centre, and a sixpence with a hole in it.

Ralph eyed the ornament with great curiosity. "Where did you get that thing?"

"It was given me."

"I wish it had been gived to me, and the sixpence along with it."

"Uncle Peter gave me that."

"Is that Peter Hambly who lives near us?"

"Yes."

"I don't like him—because—"

"Why don't you?"

"Because he talks Bible to me."

A pained look flitted over Gracie's face.

"O Ralph!" she whispered, "if you only read that, perhaps you'd be happier."

"Does you read it?"

"Yes."

"And does it make you happy?"

"Yes; I love it."

"But isn't it all about burning fire, where the bad folks go?"

"No; there's a lot more."

"I'm thinking—" said Ralph, very slowly.

"Well, what is it?"

" I'm thinking it'll be a good thing to see Aunt Poll burnt up."

" O Ralph! if you only wouldn't say such words; I can't like you when you do."

" I'll not call you Humpty Dumpty, never again."

" You'd better not," said Frank fiercely.

" Look here," said Gracie, ". shall I read you a story; it's Sunday evening, and so you can't do better than sit down here."

" Very well, do!" said Ralph, throwing himself down on the sandy floor of Gracie's rock-chamber; and then she opened her little Bible and read the history of Noah's ark, explaining it simply as she went on.

" That's a fine story," said Ralph; " I'd like to have seen those beasts going into the ark."

" That's the first ship that ever was made, isn't it, Gracie?" asked Frank.

" I think so," said Gracie; " but what I like to think is, that God kept Noah so safe while everybody else was drowned; I like to remember that when father's out on the water."

THE STORY IN THE COVE.

"What book is that tale in?" asked
Ralph, after a long pause.

" In the Bible," replied Gracie simply.

" Well, now, that's odd."

" Ralph, I wish you'd come to the Sunday school with us," said Gracie.

" *Me* go to Sunday school ! " said Ralph, with a laugh.

" Yes—you," answered Gracie earnestly; "and then you'd learn about plenty of these stories."

" No, no ; I'll come here at odd times, and you may read us a bit if it's all as good as that last. And I must be off now, I'm thinking."

" We must all be going home," said Gracie, rising and taking her crutch.

" I say, Ralph," said Frank, " are those sea-gulls' eggs hard to get ? "

" No, not a bit of it," said Ralph ; " easy enough when you know the place. But I can tell you where there's some without going to the Point—out at Gull Rock," pointing to a dark rock out in the sea at some little distance. And the cloud went off Frank's sunny face.

CHAPTER V.

ADRIFT!

" Oh, well for the fisherman's boy
    That he shouts with his sister at play;
Oh, well for the sailor lad
    That he sings in his boat on the bay."

"COME, mother; let this child out a bit," said Jacob Williams, one bright day soon after the scenes recounted in our last chapter. " She's been working hard. It's only fair she should play."

" It's time she should work," said Dame Williams, looking up. " She'll grow up a good-for-nought, helpless lass if she doesn't."

" Well, let her out to-day," said her father, smiling at the pleasure which was lighting up Gracie's face at the thought of a holiday.

"You may go, Gracie; but be back before sundown to take the baby," said her mother.

And Gracie rose with a joyous face, put away her knitting, tied on her bonnet, and then set off in search of Frank. He was at no great distance, for she soon saw him playing with Ralph on the rocks; but directly he caught sight of her he bounded over to her with a shout.

"Well done, Gracie! Is that plague of a sock put away? I'd rather go barefoot all my days than that you should always be at them."

"I've got a holiday, Frank. Where shall we go?"

"Down to the rocks, near Uncle Peter's."

"But he's out fishing."

"Never mind; we'll go to the rocks."

Gracie complied as usual, and Ralph went with them.

When they had reached the little landing-place where Uncle Peter's small white

boat was moored, Frank came close up to
Gracie, and throwing one arm round her
neck, said coaxingly, " Gracie, Ralph can
row beautifully.   Will you just get in here
for a little while, and let us have one little
pull."

" O Frank, what would Uncle Peter
say ?"

" We'll be back before he comes in, and
then he won't mind."

" But do you think father would let us ?"

" Yes ; we aren't babies now ; and Ralph
is a big boy, and he can pull, and we'll be
all safe."

" I don't think it's right, Frank."

" Oh do, Gracie ; just for me—just because I ask you."

How could she refuse when those beautiful eyes were looking so beseechingly up
into her face ?

" Well, just for a very little way," said
Gracie.   " But I'm afraid it's not right,
Frank."

"It can't be any harm," said Frank, springing into the boat; and then Gracie was helped into her seat in the stern, and Ralph took the oars.

On, on they went dancing over the water, and Gracie soon forgot, in the delight of the boating, that she had said they would only go a very little way.

"Shall we go to the Gull Rock?" said Ralph, when they had got some distance from the shore.

"Oh yes, yes," said Frank, longing to get the much-coveted eggs.

Half-an-hour's pulling brought them up to the rock; and running the boat into a little creek, the two boys sprang out of it.

"What will you do, Gracie?" asked Frank.

"I'll stay here," said Gracie. "I'll sit in the boat while you go and get the eggs. But make haste, please; because I must be back before sundown."

"Oh yes; we'll be very quick."

"The gulls' eggs are round the other
side," said Ralph.

"Is the boat safe here?" asked Gracie,
looking rather anxiously at her position.

"Oh yes; and the tide is still coming
in," said Ralph. "We'll be back before it's
turned."

"All right;" and the little girl leaned
back in the seat, and made herself quite
comfortable, to wait for them.

It was very pleasant lying there, and
watching the birds curling and flying above
her, and the waves coming up over the
rocks, and the little fishing-boats far out at
sea, while the evening sun poured a flood of
glorious light over everything. But Gracie
began to fear, after some time, that they
would be too late in getting home, and to
watch anxiously for the arrival of the boys.
Her anxiety was greatly increased by feeling the boat moving a little. She thought
it had been drawn up to high-water mark;
but on looking down she saw the water all

around her, and perceived that she most
certainly was further from the rock than
she had been at first.   And now every wave
seemed to be sending her further and further.
She tried to seize a rock that was jutting
out into the water ; but it was useless, for
the waves washed over it just as she stretched
her arms out towards it, and the boat was
further from it than ever.   In another minute
she would be past all the rocks, and out on
the wide sea !

"Frank !" she cried, as loudly as she
could.   "O Frank, come !"

But it was only a dismal echo from the
rocks which repeated her words,—" Frank,
come !" and another wave sent her further
out to sea.

She burst into tears, and covered her face
with her hands.   But crying could do no
good ; and she began at last to try and
discover in which direction the tide was
carrying her.   Alas ! it was away from the
shore ; and when they were outside their

own little cove the sea was rough and stormy.

"Oh, why, why did I do it?" sobbed the frightened child. "I knew it was wrong, and I ought to have been firm; and now I shall be drowned most likely, and then, oh, what will become of me when my last act was disobedient! And Frank, poor Frank, is on that rock, and he will starve, and no one will know where he is; and mother and father will watch for us to come back, and we shall never come. Oh, what shall I do?"

And then Gracie clasped her hands and prayed. She prayed for forgiveness for every sin in the name of her Saviour; she prayed that she might be saved from this fearful peril; and that if not, she might be taken to heaven for her Saviour's sake. But oh, above all things, she prayed that Frank might be saved. What *would* mother do if he was dead! And as long as she could she prayed for him. Then she leaned back in the boat, which she felt was being

ADRIFT!

carried further and further out to sea. The sun had set, and darkness had come on. The moon, however, was beginning to rise, and the stars to come out one by one; but the waves were stormy enough, and every now and then a shower of spray drenched the poor little girl. She began to get very stiff and cold; and she found that she could not stretch herself out, she was so cramped. And on went the boat dancing over the water, as if glad to be free from all control.

By degrees a pleasanter feeling began to
creep over little Gracie. She felt drowsy,
the pain of cramp and stiffness had gone
away, and she thought, as she laid her head
down on the edge of the boat, that she
heard murmurs in her ears like angels'
voices calling her. The moon was shining
out above her, and the stars seemed to look
down upon her with friendly eyes. She no
longer thought of the grief in her home, or
of Frank's danger, but only how pleasant it
was to lie there, and how sorry she should
be to be roused by any one. And then—
she thought no more. The moonlight shone
down upon the little white boat, and the
still whiter face resting on one of its seats,
and the waves carried the boat up and
down, and sometimes washed over it sides
a little ; but Gracie moved not—spoke not
—and did not even feel, as she was drifted,
on and on, into the great, restless, heaving
ocean.

CHAPTER VI.

THE RETURN OF THE FISHING-BOAT.

" Oh, is it weed, or fish, or floating hair?
A tress of golden hair,
O' drownèd maiden's hair,
Above the nets at sea."

"IT'S a wild night, Michael—it's a wild night, though it's fine," said an old fisherman, who stood on the deck of his little fishing-smack looking over the stormy sea.

" Yes, we can't do much," replied the other.

" Nothing, lad, nothing," said the old man. " I'm glad we've no nets out."

" Yes ; look at that old chap asleep," said the younger speaker, pointing to an old gray-haired and weather-beaten man who was lying on the deck, with his head resting on a coil of rope.

"Yes, lad, he's getting on in years like myself," said Joseph Pendrid, as he struck a light and began to fill his pipe with tobacco.

"It's a fine moon," remarked Michael, looking up.

"It is," replied Joseph; and then both men stood in silence for some moments looking out over the "watery waste."

At last Joseph said hurriedly, "Michael, lad, you've younger eyes than mine. Look there—look out yonder. D'ye see anything?" and he pointed towards a small object on the water, which the moonlight revealed distinctly.

"It's a boat, and it's drifting towards us," said Michael. "I suppose some poor neighbour's boat has got loosed from the shore, and is being driven away to sea; and as it is coming right up against us, we'll stop it."

The boat came nearer and nearer, until at last it got alongside of the fishing-smack. The moon shone directly upon it, and the fisherman perceived that it was half full of water.

" It's uncommon like Peter Hambly's little *Sea Gull*," said Joseph, as Michael was endeavouring to fasten it to their vessel. But while he was doing so, a cry of surprise broke from him.

" Joseph—Joseph Pendrid ! Look here, old man ! What's this ? " and he pointed to something which floated in the water; and then, on looking more closely, he cried, " It's a dead child ! O Joseph, look here. Her head resting on the seat, her bonnet's washed away, and this is her hair," and he lifted up the mass of Gracie's golden hair, which had fallen about her; and then the young man gently lifted the child out of the boat, and handed her up to Joseph.

" Well, here's a sorry sight," said the old man tenderly, as he sat down with the poor little girl in his arms. "You poor lamb, perhaps there's a father's heart a-breaking for you," and he looked mournfully down upon the white face, and wrung the water out of the fair hair, while Michael secured the boat.

At last Joseph cried out, "Peter! wake up, will ye, Peter—Peter Hambly!" and the old man who was sleeping on the deck roused himself, and looked up in sleepy wonder.

"Come here, Peter. Here's a poor little drowned maiden washed up against us in a half-swamped boat."

Old Peter rose as quickly as he could, and came over to Joseph's side. Then bending down, he looked long and earnestly into the face of the lifeless child. It was a strange sight : the moonlight streaming down upon the stormy water, the little fishing-smack, the rugged faces of the fishermen, and that strangely still and marble white face, with the long damp hair hanging

about it.   At last Peter Hambly spoke in
a low, broken voice, " It's Gracie—it's my
little Sunbeam ! "

" IT'S GRACIE—IT'S MY LITTLE SUNBEAM "

" Do you mean Jacob's Gracie ? " said
Joseph.

" Yes," replied Peter, taking the child
from his arms, and holding her closely in his
own.   Then, looking up suddenly, he said,
" Hush, will ye.   Stop—she lives !   Joseph,

old friend, she lives! The Almighty be thanked!"

Uncle Peter wrapped a warm coat of his own round her, and then called to Michael to bring him a small bottle of spirits which he knew was in the locker, and hastily putting some into a little horn mug, he poured it down the throat of the child; after which he chafed her cold hands, and eagerly watched for her to open her eyes.

At last she did so, slowly and heavily; and looking wonderingly into Uncle Peter's face, she said, "Where am I?"

"Safe, dearie; quite safe, with Uncle Peter," said the old man joyfully, and pressing her closer and more tightly in his arms.

"The night is cold and dark. I am wet."

"Yes, child; but lie still. You'll soon be warmer and drier."

"Shall I be drowned?"

"No, no, my dear; not if I knows it."

"How was it? I forget," and the little girl's voice was dreamy and bewildered.

"Never mind, dearie. You were in the boat, and we picked you out, that's all."

A look of recollection passed over her pale face.

"Oh, I know, I remember it all now; and Frank—O Uncle Peter! Frank's on the rock, and he'll die! Won't you go and take him off?"

"Yes, my dear, in the morning we will; but it's dark now. If Frank's on the Gull Rock, he'll be safe for to-night. Lie down here, little one, and go asleep. Old Uncle Peter will take good care of his Sunbeam."

And Gracie look earnestly at him for a moment, and said, "You are quite sure we'll go to Frank in the morning?"

"Yes, dearie."

Then the child looked satisfied, and clasping her arms round his neck, laid her head on his shoulder, and was fast asleep before many minutes had passed.

Uncle Peter sat quietly holding her for some time, and thinking how marvellous were the ways of that God who had guided the little boat over the stormy sea, and brought the child through the perils of the deep into safe keeping. And then the good old man began wondering how Gracie had come to be in the boat at all; and after turning it over several times in his own mind, he settled that it was sure to be some trick of that young cub Ralph Lennox's, and that that boy was certainly not born to be drowned, for the good reason that he would in all probability be hanged instead. When he found that Gracie was sound asleep, he carried her gently over to a quiet corner of the deck, laid her on a sail which he spread out, and then wrapped a large piece of tarpaulin over her, lashing it down, to keep her warm.

It was thus the morning sun found her, when it shone out warm and bright over the sea. The storm had abated, and the

waves were stilled, and the fishing-smack
was "homeward bound." Gracie lay quiet
for some time, thinking over all the strange
events of the night before. Presently Uncle
Peter came to her, and stooped down to
unfasten the rope which lashed the covering
over her.

"Well, Gracie, you didn't think to find
yourself a prisoner in your old uncle's boat,
did ye?"

"No, uncle," said Gracie, and her voice was
low and ashamed, her eyes filled with tears.

"What is it, dearie? You know you're
safe."

"Yes; but—"

"Well, what?" said the old man, helping
her up, and giving her the crutch which
he had just found in the bottom of the boat.

"O Uncle Peter, I've been *such* a
naughty, bad girl!" and the poor child
began to cry most bitterly.

"Come, come, Sunbeam, this won't do.
Don't, my dear, I don't like it;" and Uncle

Peter tried to remove the hands in which Gracie had hidden her tearful face. " What is it you've done ?"

" We got into your boat when you were away, and—and went to Gull Rock—and then I was waiting, and I was drifted away. O Uncle Peter, *do* forgive me," she sobbed.

" Who's *we?*" said Uncle Peter.

" Ralph, and Frank, and I; but I was worst, because I could have stopped it and didn't."

" I knew that chap was at the bottom of it," said the old fisherman.

" O Uncle Peter, it wasn't more him than us.   But oh, please forgive me; don't be angry with me, please don't."

There was a merry twinkle in the old man's eye as he replied,—

" Why, Gracie, child, did you fancy that I thought ye perfect ?"

" No, no, Uncle Peter; but have you forgiven me ?"

" Yes, yes, child, now that you're safe,

I'll forgive ye; if you'd been drowned I never would," and Uncle Peter shook his head and tried to look very fierce; then stooping down he kissed the little girl, and added, seriously, "It shows us, lass, how careful we must be; how easily we all of us may fall into sin. Let it make you more watchful, more prayerful, more humble. There, that's all the scolding the old man means to give you; only next time you want to go out boating in the *Sea Gull*, give notice to Peter Hambly, and he'll be proud to make you welcome to it, with or without his company, as you may think best."

Then Gracie saw that it was all right, and she was content.

"Uncle Peter," she said at length, "are we near the Gull Rock?"

"No, dearie; we were there before you woke this morning."

"O uncle, and Frank—is he safe?"

"I hope so, for there were no tracks of him there."

Gracie's face fell.

"Look where we are, lass;" and on turning round the little girl saw that they were just coming into the harbour at Hardrick Cove.

"Look, who's waiting for you on the beach?" said Uncle Peter.

And Gracie cried out joyfully, "Oh, it's father, and—and—yes! it *is* Frank; Uncle Peter, look, it's Frank."

At the same moment there was a joyful sound from the shore.

"Father, here's our Gracie! Gracie!— Gracie!" and Frank could hardly be kept from running through the surf to reach his sister.

A few minutes more, and Jacob Williams clasped his little daughter in his arms. "Father, please forgive me," whispered Gracie, pressing her cheek close to his.

"Yes, my child; yes, I will—you've had enough to bear, poor lamb; only, don't frighten us so again!"

"Frank, how did you get back?" asked Gracie, looking down from her exalted position upon her little brother, who was trotting along by his father's side, holding on to the end of his coat.

"We came to look for you, and you were gone; and we couldn't see you, and we thought we should die there; and Simon Lennox came late in the night and took us home in his boat. He said he knew pretty well where to look for Ralph."

"Will mother be angry?" whispered Gracie to her father.

"No, no, child." And then Dame Williams appeared at the door, looking out to see if there were any signs of their return. When she saw Gracie in her father's arms, a hearty "Thank God!" burst from her; and though she had prepared a frown by the time they reached her, yet the joyous satisfaction written on her broad face was unmistakable.

"Please, mother, I'm so sorry," said Gracie.

" Indeed, I hope you are, you naughty girl, for giving us all this worry," said the worthy dame.

" Now, mother, don't worret the child. ' She was lost, and is found;' let that be enough for us, and make us thankful for the rest of our days," said her husband.

Dame Williams's countenance relaxed, and the tears gathered in her eyes, as she held out her arms to Gracie, who sprung into them; and the kiss which passed between the mother and daughter told of complete reconciliation.

They were soon seated at breakfast, during the course of which Gracie looked up quietly and asked Frank how many gulls' eggs he had found at the rock; and Frank looked very sheepish, hung down his head, and answered, " None!"

CHAPTER VII.

HASTE TO THE RESCUE !

"Man the life-boat ! man the life-boat !
    Help, or yon ship is lost !
Man the life-boat ! man the life-boat !
    See how she's tempest-tossed.

"Life-saving ark—yon doomèd barque
    Immortal souls doth bear ;
Nor gems, nor gold, nor wealth untold,
    But *men, brave* men, are there."

HE next few weeks passed away very quietly in Gracie's home. The children had had a fright, and its effects were visible for some time. Gracie was quiet and subdued, and Frank was less wild and mischievous, and clung to his sister with warmer love than ever. Ralph, too, was not the same boy that he had formerly been, for his intercourse with Gracie

had softened his rough ways, and given him
fresh interests and pleasures. His great
delight was to find curious things for Gracie,
and bring them to her to ornament her cove;
and his knowledge of all the places around
helped him in this. Frank used often to
accompany him in his wild searches after
sea-birds' eggs, rare sea-weeds and shells,
or pebbles to lay down as a flooring in
the rock-chamber; and though Jacob Williams sometimes watched in fearfulness and
anxiety the growing friendship between the
two boys, he trusted very much to Gracie's
influence to counteract the bad effects of
companionship with Ralph, while he felt
that the wild neglected boy might perhaps
be kept from much that was evil by asso-
ciating with his children.

Gracie's life went on very quietly; her
daily round of household duties was per-
formed patiently and steadily, and her
gentle influence for good was very percep-
tible. She seemed to live with the one

thought always uppermost, how she might show her love to Him who had shown such wondrous love to her; and this ruling motive seemed to brighten everything she did. No action was too small to come under its power, and it lightened every cross, and made every trial less painful to her.

It was about six weeks after that night of adventure which we told of in the last chapter, and the day had been one of rain and wind.

The leaden colour of the sky was reflected in the sea, except where the white foam of the crested waves broke the monotonous gray, and the noise of the breakers on the shore was like that of great guns booming. The fisher's boats were all safely moored in the harbour, for "nothing could live in such a sea," they said; and the fishermen themselves were mending their nets, or playing with their children in their various homes.

It was drawing towards evening, and

Gracie's work was finished; the baby was asleep in its cradle, the dame was preparing the evening meal, Frank was making a net by the fire, and Jacob sat near the cottage window with one arm round his little daughter, whose head was resting on his shoulder as she stood by his side.

The wind howled in fury as it swept past the cottage door, an occasional peal of thunder rent the air, and a vivid flash of lightning lit up the seething, restless water.

"O father, it's a terrible night," said Gracie fearfully, as they looked out at the wild scene before them in the dim twilight.

"It is, my lass; you must pray for those at sea."

Gracie's arm tightened round his neck, as if she would, by that means, express her thankfulness for *his* safety.

"Should you be 'feared, lass, if you were out to-night?" said Jacob.

"I don't know, daddy; I should think of something."

A STORMY NIGHT.

" What should you think of?"
Gracie hesitated, but at length she re-

plied, in a low voice, " What Mr. Trelawney preached about last Sunday."

" What was that ? " said her father.   And Gracie answered,—

" Of Him who is ' the confidence of them that are afar off upon the sea ;......which stilleth the noise of the seas, the noise of their waves, and the tumult of the people.' "

" Quite right, my lass," answered her father ; " I often think of that when I'm out."

They were silent for a few minutes, listening to the fury of the sounds which were mingling outside the cottage.   At last Jacob spoke,—

" I remember when I was a youngster my mother once read me something about a storm out of the Bible, but I've never found the place since, though it was a very true and a good bit."

" I wonder if it was what Mrs. Trelawney was teaching us on Sunday last," said Gracie, " because that's exactly like this evening."

" Can you say it, lass ? "

" I think so," replied Gracie, and, after pausing for a few moments, she repeated it. ' The waters saw thee, O God, the waters saw thee; they were afraid : the depths also were troubled. The clouds poured out water; the skies sent out a sound : thine arrows also went abroad. The voice of thy thunder was in the heaven : the lightnings lightened the world: the earth trembled and shook. Thy way is in the sea, and thy path in the great waters, and thy footsteps are not known. ' "

" It's very true; the men that wrote that had seen a storm, I'll warrant," said her father, as he stroked her hair when she had done.

" I should think so," replied Gracie. " O daddy, look ; d'ye see ? "

" See what, child ? "

" Look ! those two ; " and Gracie pointed to a couple of figures, dimly seen in the gloom of the evening light, who were stealing stealthily along the shore.

" I see," muttered Jacob half to himself;
" it's Kenrick the wrecker, and Poll Lennox. They are up to no good, child."

Gracie knew quite enough of the evil
ways and cruel actions of the wreckers to
guess her father's meaning ; but she did not
answer, for at this moment a vivid flash of
lightning lit up the whole scene, and was
quickly succeeded by a loud crash of
thunder. After this, for a few seconds,
there seemed to be a lull in the storm ; tho
wind abated, the waves broke more gently,
and then distinctly above them there rose a
sound which made Jacob start to his feet,
and Gracie clasp her hands in terror.

" O father !" she cried, " what was it ? "

" Hush !" said her father, laying his
finger on his lips and listening intently ; but
the wind swept past the window with a wild
shriek, and the angry waves broke with a
louder roar than ever, as if, in that momen-
tary lull, they had been gathering fresh
strength and fury. Then there was seen

over the sea for one instant a bright flash, and Jacob cried, "God have mercy on them; it is a ship in distress;" and he seized his sou'-wester from the nail on the wall, snatched up his pea-jacket, and opened the cottage door.

"Jacob, good-man, don't ye go," said his wife, coming hastily forward; "no boat can live in such a sea. Don't ye go for to risk *your* life. Think of me and these poor children."

"Hold your peace, dame. Think you I'll sit in my house while poor souls are perishing in the wild waters, and I've a hand to save them? I knew it was not for nothing that those beggarly wreckers were sneaking about."

"Father," said Gracie, throwing her arms round his neck, "come back; oh, do!"

"Yes, yes, my lass; what were those words? say them, — 'The confidence of them—'"

"'That are afar off upon the sea,'" whis-

pered Gracie.   " He will take care of you ;
I know he will."

"Bless you, my child.   And, Gracie, if I
don't come back, take care of your mother, and
be a comfort to her ;" and then he kissed
her, and walked off through the darkness
and the wind and rain in the direction of
the harbour, where already a knot of fishermen were gathering.

After her father had gone, Gracie moved
restlessly from the door to the window,
then to the fireplace, and then back again
to the window.   " Mother," she said at last,
coming round to her mother's side, " the
rain has nearly ceased, the moon is rising.
O mother, come to the harbour ; I want to
watch father's boat ; I know he's gone out,
—it was in his face that he would."

"Yes, yes, mother, come down to the
harbour," cried Frank, who had long ago
thrown aside his netting, and was leaning on
the window-seat, gazing out very longingly
in the direction of the harbour, and wishing

vainly that he was a man, that he might go into the midst of the danger.

" Baby is asleep," whispered Gracie ; " O mother, come ; " and the little girl's voice was tremulous with eagerness.

The good woman's heart was yearning to know something of her husband, and she rose quickly, threw a cloak around her and over her head, put on Frank's cap, and taking a hand of each child, locked the cottage door behind her, and set off in the direction of the harbour.

The storm was certainly abating, the rain had ceased, and the moon was struggling to come out from behind its covering of dark and stormy clouds, and distinctly above the sound of the howling wind and the furious waves was heard that solitary booming gun, more heart-rending than the most piercing cry of distress that ever passed from mortal lips.

At length they reached the harbour, and Dame Williams eagerly inquired after her husband.

" Ay," replied old Joseph Pendrid, shaking his head, " you may well ask for him,
dame ; ask them waves, and they'll tell ye."

" He would go," said another man ; " we
told him how it would be.   Look, dame,
there's the wreck ; " and he pointed out to a
dark object which seemed sometimes to be
engulfed by the waves, and sometimes was
lifted high upon the top of them.

" But—speak—tell me, he isn't drowned ?
Speak, can't ye ! " said the poor woman in
terror.

" We saw the boat go out, he and two
more chaps in it ; but we haven't seen it
since, and nothing could stand against this
sea," replied Joseph.

Gracie stood quietly by her mother's side,
clasping her hand tightly, and straining her
eyes " across the stormy water," endeavouring to catch sight of her father's boat.   It
was a terrible time of suspense, but suddenly
there arose a joyful cry, " It's safe there,
and it's coming back ; God speed them ! "

And, true enough, the moonlight shone down clearly and brightly over the water, and showed the little boat, as full as it could hold, high on the crest of an immense wave. It was lost to sight again directly; but a long and loud cheer broke from the whole crowd, and a faint kind of echo seemed to come from the sea. And now it came nearer and nearer to the harbour, though each wave seemed threatening to over-whelm it.

"It's safe!" shouted two or three; but Joseph shook his head, and pointed to a large wave just gathering over it. Again it was lost to sight, and a wild, bitter cry came up from the sea.

"Lost! lost!" cried Joseph; "that wave has done for them."

"No! no!" cried a child's voice, clearly rising above the din and confused murmur of the voices all round. " I know he's safe —look!" and they did look, and then a shout arose, "Gracie, you're right—they're safe;"

and there was the little boat close under
them, brought safely into the haven where
it would be.

"All safe?" cried Joseph.

"Two men and a woman washed overboard before; eight saved," replied Jacob,
as the rescued mariners sprang to the shore;
and then, having secured the boat, he followed them quietly, and stood amongst
them with his honest, brave face a little
brighter than usual, but otherwise unmoved.

"Take care of these good fellows," he said
cheerily, as his neighbours flocked around
him, pouring out their congratulations and
praise, and eager to testify their approbation
of his conduct by a hearty squeeze of his
hand; "they've had cold water enough for
one night, give them something warmer now.
Why, little daughter, *you* here!" he added,
as his eyes fell upon Gracie, who was pressing forward to meet him.

"Yes; and mother and Frank," cried
Gracie, when she had reached him.

"Thank God," said the dame, raising her apron to her eyes, "you're safe, Jacob. Come home now and change your things."

And Jacob, taking his little daughter's hand, turned in the direction of his own home, while a loud cheer arose from the fishermen.

JACOB'S RETURN.

The good dame was, in no small degree, gratified by this token of esteem for her husband, and turning round, she cried, "Thank ye, neighbours; we're very much

obliged to ye all.   May ye all be as brave
men and as good husbands as my Jacob,
though I say it as shouldn't."

A loud laugh and still louder cheer followed this speech.

" Why do they cheer ? " asked Frank.

" Only because I've done my duty," replied his father, as they reached the cottage
door, and the cheering died away in the distance.

For one moment Gracie and her father
lingered to look out over the sea, and stooping down, he said to her in a low, earnest
voice,—

" ' The waves of the sea are mighty, and
rage horribly; but yet the Lord, who
dwelleth on high, is mightier.'   O Gracie,
child, never till this night did I know the
full blessedness of having him for my confidence when I was ' afar off upon the sea.' "

CHAPTER VIII.

THE WRECKER'S PRIZE.

"Or if He see fit that our boat should sink,
  By a storm, or a leak, like lead;
Yet still of the glorious day we'll think,
  When the sea shall yield her dead.
For they who depart in his faith and fear
  Shall find their passage is short,
From the troublesome waves that beset life here,
  To the everlasting port."

THE next day Gracie was sitting in her little cove, knitting and singing to herself, though she could hardly hear her own voice above the noise of the waves, which had not quieted down entirely, though their fury was much abated.

The little girl's heart was full of thankfulness for her father's preservation, and pleased and proud because every one was praising him; and Mr. Trelawney had that

morning come down from the Rectory and
asked all about the wreck, and shaken hands
with her father, and wished that he could
have shared his glory.

The *Polly Ann*—for such was the name of
the unfortunate vessel—was lying on one side
out in the water.   It was now only a miserable hulk, and a sad object it looked ; but
the lives of eight of its crew were saved.

It was a small trading vessel, which was
going round from one of the southern ports
to the coast of Wales, and had been driven
out of its course by contrary winds.

Gracie had never seen an actual wreck
before, and it made a strong impression upon
her ; and while her heart was full of grati-
tude about her father, she could not help
thinking of the three poor souls who had
been washed overboard, and wondering as to
what could be their fate.

Frank was with his father down in the
harbour, and so Gracie sat by herself and
sung ; for the louder the waves roared, the

more she enjoyed trying to raise her voice above them. But she was interrupted by hearing some one saying her name close to her, and turning her head, she saw David Kenrick leaning over the rock behind her.

Gracie's thoughts flew back to the evening before, when she saw him, like some bird of prey, ready to seize upon any unfortunate victims, and strip them of their possessions, and she involuntarily shrunk from him.

"Grace," he repeated in a louder tone; and then she answered slowly,—

"Well?"

"It was a wild storm last night."

"It was," replied Gracie, knitting faster than ever.

"Your father spoilt our profit."

"Oh, don't, don't speak like that," said Gracie, shuddering; "you can't mean it."

"Mean what, lass?"

"Why, that you wanted—that you would have liked those poor men to be drowned, that you might get their clothes and things

when they were washed up," she answered
hesitatingly.

"Well, I don't know that exactly—I can't
swear to that; but when they are drowned
I don't see that this world's goods can do
much for them."

"No! but still—"

"Well, child, don't you see dead folks
don't want clothes and food, and living ones
do; that's all the difference;" and the man's
dark countenance grew a shade darker as
he spoke, and after a moment's silence he
added,—"It don't signify what *I* do. I
may as well make my living that way as
another; there's no one to care."

Gracie's eyes swam with tears, and lifting
her face from her work, she said gently,
"Oh, for Abel's sake, don't do it!"

A quick sharp look of pain passed over
the man's face, and his voice had a slight
huskiness in it as he answered, "That minds
me of what I came here for. Will ye come
with me?"

Gracie started. "Why?" she asked rather fearfully.

"Well, I'll tell you. Last night the water washed up a poor creature from the wreck, not quite dead, but nearly so. Poll Lennox would soon have dispatched her; but I wouldn't have it, for there was something in the woman's face that reminded me of my boyish days. She was all dressed in rags, and had a child in her arms; but the poor baby was dead, and the woman's dying fast. She's lying in the little ruined hut, down along the shore towards the Point; and now she's come to, she's moaning and crying out."

"But why should *I* go?" asked Gracie.

"Well, the poor thing knows she's dying, and she's been calling out to know if it's true that there's any one to save a dying soul; and she says the Name that Abel used to say, and wants to hear if it's true; and I said I'd come and look you up, because you'd know all about it."

THE WRECKER'S PRIZE.

"But mother's out; and I don't know if I may."

"I'll take care of you, child," said Kenrick gravely; "the poor thing hasn't much longer to hold out—come now."

"Why didn't you go and fetch Mr. Trelawney?"

"Well, I don't think I'm likely to do that," said Kenrick, with a laugh, "though he's a good man too is that parson, and a gentleman as well; but he's been a-talking to me, and I'm not going to bring him about my places. Will ye come, little Gracie?"

"Yes," said Gracie, trembling; and she rose and followed Kenrick along the shore until they reached the hut. Her fears increased when she saw Poll Lennox in the corner of it, tying up in a bundle some of the spoils collected from the last night's storm.

In one corner of the hut, stretched on a piece of tarpaulin, lay a woman whose wasted features and short quick breathing told that death was not far from her; and in her arms she clasped a dead child, whose little white face bore a sweet, calm look, very unlike that of its wretched mother, whose restless, wandering eyes seemed to be looking round vainly in search of comfort and hope.

"Here's Gracie Williams," said Kenrick, approaching her side, and leading Gracie up; "she can tell you."

"Tell me—tell me what?" asked the woman, raising herself. "Can she tell me when my child will awake—tell me when my husband will come from the sea again?"

"No, no," said Gracie. "I'm so sorry you are ill, I want to do anything I can for you."

"It's too late, too late; it's all too late," said the woman wildly. "Tell me," she cried, clasping her child closer to her, "is there any one who can save?"

Gracie's tongue seemed tied; she knew not what to say; but she silently prayed for strength, and then answered slowly, "The Bible says, 'Jesus Christ came into the world to save sinners.'"

" Are you sure ? " asked the poor sufferer.

" Quite, quite sure ; and it says, ' The blood of Jesus Christ cleanseth us from all sin.' "

" Oh, I know it, I know it ; I heard it long ago. Read me of Him ;" and she took from her bosom a little book wrapped up, and feebly handing it to Gracie, lay back faint and exhausted. It was a New Testament, and Gracie read of the love of the Saviour to all who would come to him.

" Read me of the two sons—the one that ran away," whispered the woman with difficulty.

Gracie turned to the 15th of St. Luke, and began reading the history of the prodigal son ; but she had not got far before the woman uttered a long piercing cry of " Father, O my father !" and fell back in a faint."

" I'll go and look for more assistance," said Gracie, taking her crutch and rising.

" Make haste," said Poll Lennox, who

was supporting the dying woman, and Grace set off.

She had not got far before she spied the well-known figure of Uncle Peter coming to meet her.

"Well, Gracie, child," he said, "here I am come all this way to look for ye; and some one told me you'd been walking along with Kenrick the wrecker—bad company for you," and he shook his head at her playfully. But he soon saw that something was the matter, for she could hardly speak, but seized his hand and drew him on in the direction of Kenrick's hut.

"Come, Uncle Peter, come! she's dying— a poor woman from the wreck, and I don't know how to speak to her rightly; come."

Uncle Peter hurried after her as fast as he could, and they had soon reached the hut, and found that the poor woman had recovered from the faint, and was looking round for Gracie.

But no sooner did her eyes fall upon

Uncle Peter, than she stretched her arms out to him, and in an instant he was kneeling by her side, sobbing like a child, while the woman's cry of " Father ! father !" told that Uncle Peter's lost one had returned, and that Mary would be forgiven and comforted before she died.

" FATHER ! FATHER !"

" Father, I have sinned," she whispered.

" O my girl ! my daughter ! you've come home ; all the past is forgot. My God, this is *thy* mercy!" and then Uncle Peter's voice failed him.

"Father," she went on, "I was coming back to you some time. Richard said he would bring me. I was wretched for years after I went, and yet I could not get back. I went to America, and there I found my happiness; for after I'd been a servant some years I married him—my Richard, my brave, good Richard—him that the cruel sea took from me last night; and we were come back to England, and were going to Wales to his father, and he said he'd bring me to you some day—and he was so good!—O father, I did not deserve him. But God gave him to me; and my child—look, father, my little dead baby; Richard had him called Peter for your sake, though he never saw you. And then the storm came, and he was trying to save me, and we were both washed over, and they say he's drowned—O father, father!"

"My poor lamb," said the old man tenderly, as he laid his hand on her head; "my poor dear child."

"Father, *pray*," she whispered; "pray God to forgive me for Jesus Christ's sake, as you used to do when I was a child by your knee."

Then the old man knelt, and Gracie knelt, and Kenrick the wrecker knelt too (Poll Lennox had stolen away), and earnestly and simply the old man prayed for the parting soul of his child; and as he prayed, a look of peace stole over her face—a look resembling that of the dead child by her side.

"Forgiven!" she whispered when he had done; "forgiven for His sake, saved through Him. Kiss me, father; say *you* forgive me; bless me."

"God Almighty bless you, my daughter. I forgive ye as I hope to be forgiven, and soon I'll be following you to that safe haven."

"Lay me by mother and Jack, father, won't you!—and put Richard with me, and my baby."

" I will, my child," said the old man.

Mary held out her hand to Gracie. " God
bless you, dear ; will you be good to father
when I'm gone ? Is that David Kenrick
that used to play with me and Jack ? Good-
bye, David."

Then there was a long, long silence in the
little hut, only broken by the short breathing of the dying woman. At last she spoke,
or tried to say something to her father, of
which he could only catch the last words,
" Him that cometh—"

"To me, I will in no wise cast out," said
her father gently. A smile spread itself
over her face, a smile full of peace and hope ;
and then she died.

" Look here, Gracie," said Kenrick, calling her outside the cottage, and closing the
door behind him. " Look, this is her Richard ; poor Mary !" and he lifted up a sail
which was spread over something that lay
there, and showed her a man who had been
washed on shore that morning. " We haven't

touched anything of his," he added; and
Gracie looked upon the still, white features,
and the damp curly hair, and thought of
Richard and of poor Mary; and then, as
Kenrick laid the sail down again over him,
she whispered to herself, " They are together now."

CHAPTER IX.

FRANK'S WISH.

"Summer ocean! how I'll miss thee,—
 Miss the thunder of thy roar,
Miss the music of thy ripple,
 Miss thy sorrow-soothing shore!
Summer ocean! how I'll miss thee
 When 'the sea shall be no more!'"

THE grass had grown green on Mary and Richard's graves, and a year had passed away. There were not many changes in the quiet little village, however, except that old Joseph Pendrid was dead, and Uncle Peter was obliged to give up work, and lived now upon his small savings in his comfortable little cottage by the sea. His hair had grown grayer and his step more feeble, now that his last earthly hope was gone; but *all* his affections were fixed in that quiet haven where he longed to be with "those who had gone before."

It had been a calm still day, and the evening was one of extreme beauty. Gracie was sitting by his side reading to him out of his large Bible, while the old man smoked his pipe. The chapter he had asked for was in the Book of Revelation, and told of the time when the old heaven and earth were to pass away, and there was to be no more sea.

Gracie paused when she came to this, and looking up thoughtfully, she said,—

"Uncle Peter, I can't make this out; I don't like to think that we shall have no sea in heaven."

"I don't think it, lass," replied the old man.

"But it says so," said Gracie, laying her finger on the verse she had been reading.

"Well, lass, I've not much learning, but I think just this: there'll not be the same sea; no more storms, no more wrecks; we can ne'er again lose our loved ones in its angry waves, and it can never part folks more ; but, dearie, we read of a sea of glass mingled with fire, and on it harpers harping on their harps. A calm sea, lass, with no more cruel storms."

Gracie's face brightened considerably. "O Uncle Peter, I'm glad of that! I'll always think of that—a sea like this, so calm and clear, with the sunlight across it."

"No more sea," repeated Uncle Peter, half to himself. "When we've passed through the waves of this troublesome world, and have reached the quiet haven, there will be printed clear above the entrance to it that which will stop every wave of trouble, of pain, or of care from coming near the Lord's children ; for he himself will say to them, 'Hitherto shall ye come, and no further.'"

"Uncle Peter, I want to tell you something," said Gracie, when she had finished reading, and had closed the book.

" Well, dearie !"

" Do you know Frank's been so good lately ; he's so kind to me, and so good and nice at home, I think he's going to be just like our George."

" I hope so, lass ; isn't that the boy himself coming to look for you ? "

" Yes, Uncle Peter, it's him; he said he'd come to fetch me home."

And Frank approached them, whistling merrily to himself, and looking the picture of health and joy, as if the mere fact of living were a delight to him ; and any one who had seen him, would not have wondered that Gracie was proud of her brother.

" Well, Gracie, I've come," he cried, as he flung himself down on the sand by their side.

" I see you have," said Gracie, laughing ; "and I suppose I must put on my cloak, as mother will be wanting me."

" Yes, come along." And as soon as Gracie was dressed, they bid Uncle Peter goodnight, and set off on their homeward walk.

For some time Frank did not speak, but walked on whistling; at last, however, he stopped abruptly, and said,—

"Gracie, I say, haven't I been a good boy lately?"

"Yes, Frank, very," replied Gracie, smiling at the blunt way in which the question was put.

"I've done everything I've been told; I've not been mischievous; I've not let Peggy toddle down into the sea more than once; I've made a big net; and I've—"

"I know, Frank, but we shouldn't praise ourselves so much," answered his sister, laughing merrily.

"I don't care,—I just wanted to know."

"Well, I think you *have* been very good."

"Then, Gracie, don't you think," and the little boy's voice sunk to a confidential whisper, "don't you think they might let me go to the Point with Ralph?"

"No, Frank; you know daddy doesn't like you to go there."

Frank's face fell.

"I'm no baby now; I don't see why I shouldn't go—it's a famous clambering place, and there are quantities of eggs there. Gracie, I mean to ask daddy to-night."

"It'll only vex him," said Gracie gravely.

"I'll try," said Frank. "Of course it wouldn't do for a girl like you to go there, but a man ought to be able to climb anywhere."

"*A man!*" said Gracie rather mockingly.

"How you do tease one," replied Frank impatiently. "I believe it's because you can't go yourself you don't want me to have the fun."

"Frank, that's not true," said Gracie, while the bright colour mounted into her pale cheeks.

Frank was sorry in an instant, and said, "No, it's not true; you're a good Gracie;" but there was a cloud on his sunny face as they entered their cottage door.

When the evening meal was ended, and

Jacob's pipe was lit, Frank came to his side, bringing the large net he had finished that day.

"Look, father, isn't it a big one?"

"Yes, lad. Why, you're getting quite a handy little fisherman; I'll soon be taking you out in my boat."

Frank looked up joyfully.

"I'm growing a big fellow, daddy—too big to be idle, don't you think?" and he stretched his head up to see if it reached his father's shoulder when he was sitting down.

"Ay, ay, too old to be idle, my lad."

"Daddy," said Frank hesitatingly, but in a very entreating voice, "I want to ask you something."

"Well, lad, speak up."

"Will you say 'Yes'?"

"If I don't say 'No' I will," replied Jacob, taking his pipe from his mouth and shaking the ashes out of it.

"May I go along with Ralph to Sea Gull Point to-morrow?"

ASKING LEAVE.

"No!" said his father hastily but decided. "Mind my words, youngster, if I catch you going there, I'll make you remember it."

"But I'd be very careful, father," pleaded the little boy.

"Be quiet, Frank; I won't have one word of that. You're not to go; d'ye hear?"

"It's too bad," muttered the boy sullenly, as he turned into the house; and wicked rebellious thoughts rose up in his mind that night as he lay in his little bed.

The next day, Gracie was sitting at work in the afternoon on a rock near the sea, when she saw Frank come out of the cottage, looking very downcast. She called to him, and he came over to her slowly.

"What's the matter?" she said very gently, and in a sympathizing tone which Frank knew well. His lip quivered, and he turned his head away, and then she repeated her question.

A sob was the only answer she received, and gently putting her arm round her little brother's neck, she looked lovingly into his face, which he was trying vainly to conceal, that she might not see that he was crying.

"What is it, Franky?"

"I want—oh, I want to go to the Point."

"But, Frank, you know daddy knows best."

"Oh, don't preach like that; I want to go."

"Why do you want it so much; I never saw you cry for anything of that kind before?"

"Because—because Ralph thinks I'm a coward, and afraid to go there."

"But you're not, Franky dear; you need not mind what Ralph thinks, need you?"

"I can't help it," sobbed Frank.

"Oh yes, you can; now, Frank, we'll have a merry time out here this afternoon; don't go away and leave me."

Frank dried his tears.

"I'll tell you what I'll do," said Gracie, "I'll give you those sea-gull eggs that Ralph brought me; would you like them?"

"Yes," said Frank, rubbing the sleeve of his blue fustian jacket across his eyes, and brightening up considerably.

"Gracie, Gracie," cried her mother, coming to the door of the cottage, "come and take Peggy for a while; I'm afraid she'll get into mischief."

Gracie rose. "Now, Frank, wait here for me, like a good boy; I won't be long."

"All right," said Frank, seating himself on the rock she had quitted, and throwing some pebbles and pieces of broken shells down into the water below him.

Gracie meanwhile went into the cottage and asked her mother's leave to take Peggy out; and the little one held out her hand in token of her willingness to go with "Gay," as she called her sister in the peculiar baby language which she was beginning to acquire.

"Yes, you shall come, darling," said Gracie, getting down the little pink bonnet and tying it on the curly head. "Come along and play with brother;" but when she had reached the rock, Frank was gone !

CHAPTER X.

WHERE IS HE?

> " The billows swell, the winds are high,
>   Clouds overcast the wintry sky;
> Out of the depths to thee we call,
>   Our fears are great, our strength is small.
>
> " Amidst the roaring of the sea
>   Our souls still hang their hope on thee;
> Thy constant love and faithful care
>   Support, and save us from despair."

EVENING came, and Jacob Williams returned from his work.

"Where's Frank?" was his first question, as he glanced round the cottage and saw his wife, Gracie, and little toddling Peggy, but missed the merry face of his boy.

"I don't know, daddy," said Gracie, looking up; "he was with me in the early part of the afternoon, and then when I came in to fetch Peggy, he went off."

"He ought to be in, it's getting dark," said Jacob, putting down his nets in a corner.

"He's out later than this at times," said his mother.

"Let's have our tea, wife."

An hour passed, and still Frank came not.

"This is getting beyond a joke," said Jacob, rising. "Gracie, child, where do you think he is?"

"I don't know, daddy," replied the little girl fearfully.

"He couldn't have gone to the Point, could he?" said the father, while a look of terror passed over his face.

"I don't think so, father, but Ralph would know; will you step down and ask Ralph?"

"I don't think you need, for that's the boy himself coming," said his mother eagerly; but the footstep passed the door, and an anxious, terrified look settled down on the parents' faces.

"I'll be off to Simon Lennox's," said Jacob, seizing his hat, and hastily quitting the house. A few minutes' quick walking brought him to Ralph's house, and he knocked loudly at the door.

Poll Lennox opened it.

"Is your Ralph in ?" asked Jacob.

"He is, worse luck to him," replied his aunt.

"Can I speak a word to him ?"

"As many as you will, but I doubt you'll get no answer ; the boy's in a sulk, and sits there like a log."

Jacob entered the house, and, glancing round the room, saw Ralph on a low stool near the fire, with his elbows on his knees, and his chin supported by his hands, looking hard into the glowing coals. The firelight shone on his face, and showed that it was ashen pale ; his eyes had a scared and terrified look about them, and his mouth bore the impress of dogged obstinacy.

"Ralph, where's my Frank ?" said Jacob, coming up to him suddenly.

The boy gave a wild start, but when Jacob repeated his question, he only shook his head in reply, and stared straight into the fire.

"Have you been with Frank this afternoon?" asked the fisherman again.

Ralph shook his head.

"Speak, can't ye!" said his Aunt Poll, coming up to him and striking him hard across the face.

A cry of pain burst from him, and Jacob eagerly interposed: "Don't strike the lad, that'll do no good; speak, Ralph, tell me if you know anything of Frank."

But the dogged silence was still maintained.

"Ralph, I've never been unkind to you, I've let my children play with you, and be with you—tell me now the truth, where's Frank?"

Ralph looked up for one moment, and said in a loud voice, "I know nothing at all about him."

"Has he not been with you?"

" No !" and then the boy shuddered, and relapsed once more into his old position and his former silence.

" There, ye see, ye can make naught of him," said his aunt.

And Jacob turned sorrowfully away, and went home to tell the sad news to his anxious wife and poor frightened Gracie. All night he wandered up and down the shore, between the Point and his own house, calling to his boy, and thinking that everything he stumbled against was Frank's dead body. The news had fled like wildfire through the village, and many neighbours had offered their help to him. When the morning dawned Jacob returned home, weary and broken-hearted, from his fruitless search.

At the door of his cottage he met Michael, the young fisherman, who has been before mentioned in this story.

" I'm sorry for your trouble, Jacob," said the young man, who had a year-old baby at home, and knew what he himself should be feeling if anything had happened to his treasure. "It goes to my heart to see ye."

Jacob's face had changed considerably during that night of anxiety, and he now looked like a haggard old man, and the tears rushed to his eyes as Michael spoke.

"Where was the boy last seen?" asked Michael.

"On the rocks opposite our cottage," replied the father, in a low, broken voice.

"Why, man, I saw him after that," said the young fisherman musingly.

"Saw him!—where?—when?—speak, Michael Penrose."

"I saw him—now, let me see—I saw him, about four of the clock, going along the cliff above the Point—Ralph Lennox, I think it was, with him. They clambered down the rocks on to the Point, and then I didn't see him any more. I thought you must be somewhere near; you'd never let that chap go to such a place alone."

A look of the most extreme anguish

crossed the father's face. "I've asked Ralph already—he will not speak except to deny that he saw Frank at all."

"The young liar," said Michael angrily. "Come along, Jacob, and ask him again."

So they went together to Lennox's cottage. The father was in this time, and greeted them with a hoarse laugh.

"Come to make my youngster talk, have ye ?"

"Yes," said Michael; "I saw him with Frank Williams yesterday, and he shall speak. What became of him, Ralph ?" and to enforce his words, he seized the boy by the collar of his jacket, and shook him violently.

Ralph wrenched himself away from his grasp, and glared at him in anger, but did not speak.

"You'd better speak, my chap, I can tell ye," said Simon angrily, "or I'll make ye."

The boy put his hand up to his head as if bewildered, and gazed from one to another with a look of wonder.

"Speak, Ralph; there's a good lad," said Jacob earnestly.

But Ralph only shook his head again.

"Leave him alone," said Simon; "I'll make him tell, and then I'll come and let ye know."

And as Jacob and Michael walked away down the shore, they heard the sound of screaming and cries of pain, which told them that Simon was trying to extract the secret by blows.

When Jacob again reached his own home, Gracie met him on the door-step; her face was very pale and eager, and her eyes were swollen with crying.

"Well, daddy?" she cried as he came up.

Her father did not speak, but passed her quickly and went into the house.

"What is it, Michael?" asked Gracie, lingering for a moment.

"That young dog Ralph knows, but will not tell," replied Michael. "O Gracie, I fear it's very bad; you know the tide is so dangerous at the Point—and it was there he was, for I saw him."

Gracie turned away from him and entered the house. Her father was sitting by the table, with his arms leaning on it, and his face buried in them, and his whole frame was heaving with deep sobs. Dame Williams was crying loudly, but was tying on her bonnet.

" I'm going to make Ralph tell," she said hastily, as she met Gracie's inquiring look, and then she went out.

"Father," whispered Gracie, coming up close beside him, "dear, dear, father."

He did not speak, for the sound of her voice seemed only to increase his sorrow. She slipped her hand under his arm, and took one of his. "Father!" she said again.

"Oh, my boy—my boy!" sobbed Jacob; and then he raised his head, took Gracie in his arms, and the father and child wept together.

"Daddy," she said at length, clasping her

arms tightly round his neck, "God says,
'Call upon me in the time of trouble, and I
will deliver thee.'"

Jacob pressed her more closely to him,
but did not answer.

"I prayed for Frank all last night," said
Gracie.

"I could bear anything but this uncer-
tainty," muttered her father.

"Dear father, ask God to tell us one way
or the other."

"You are right, lass; we will;" and
Jacob flung himself on his knees and
prayed. It was a wild, broken prayer, but
it seemed to comfort him just to say over
and over again, "Lord, have mercy upon
us ! and tell us what to do—save my boy—
have mercy upon us !" And after this they
rose stronger and calmer.

"My best little comforter," said Jacob, as
he kissed Gracie's forehead. "And now,
child, what shall we do?—here's mother, and
I see by her face she's had no news."

" No news—that wicked boy seems as if he was possessed with a dumb devil," said the poor mother.

" Father," said Gracie very earnestly, " let me go and try. Ralph has always been good to me ; may *I* try, dear father ?"

" I don't like you to go amongst that lot," said her father.

" Oh, do let me—I'm not afraid—*do*, father."

" Well go, lass ; and the Lord prosper you. I'll get Michael to come to the Point with me."

So Gracie went over to her little treasure-box, and taking out of it Uncle Peter's six-pence and the ornament which Kenrick had given her, wrapped them up, slipped them inside her dress, and set off.

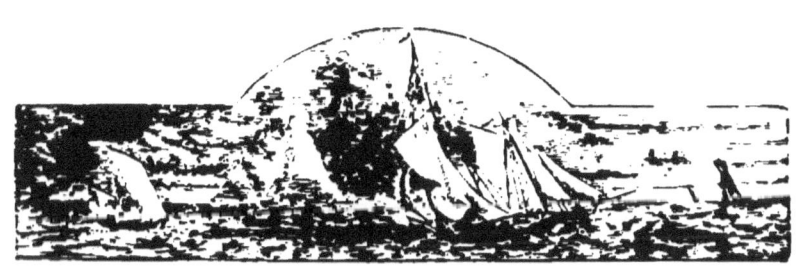

CHAPTER XI.

FALLEN OVER.

"He can save us still,
For His are the winds and the sea;
And if He is with us, we'll fear no ill,
Whatever the danger be."

RALPH was leaning against the door-post as Gracie came up to the cottage, and as soon as he saw her he turned his head away.

The little girl went close up to him, and, holding out her hand, said gently,—

"Poor Ralph, they've been beating you."

"I don't care," said Ralph sulkily, and stooping down to pick up a stone.

"I'm *so* sorry," said Gracie, in the same pitying tone which she had used to him on

that day long ago, when she had first comforted and helped him.

" You're not !" said Ralph, looking wistfully into her face.

" I am indeed," said Gracie. " Look
here, Ralph—I've brought you these things ;
you said once you'd like them ;" and she drew
the little parcel from its hiding-place.

" I don't want 'em," said Ralph.

" I'll give them both to you, if—if—" and
her voice sunk very low, " if you'll tell me
where Frank is."

" I've said I don't know," muttered Ralph.

" But you do know—you know quite
well. O Ralph, Ralph, please tell me ; I
love him, and I shall be so unhappy, and I
am so miserable—and you are miserable too
—O Ralph, tell me !" and she burst into tears.

" Don't cry," said Ralph, covering his face
with his hands ; " I can't bear it, Gracie—
don't. Oh, what shall I do ?—what shall I
do ?"

" Please—please tell me," said Gracie.

"Well, come here;" and Ralph drew her away behind the house.

Gracie trembled violently—she knew not why—but she dreaded hearing what he had got to tell.

"Do you want to know?" said Ralph.

"Yes."

"Will you not let me be hanged?" he asked, while his voice sunk to a low, mysterious whisper.

A CONFESSION.

"O Ralph, Ralph, speak; where is he?"

"I've killed him," said Ralph, while his

whole face seemed working with some great terror.

" Where is he ?" asked Gracie.

" *Fallen over*," was all Ralph's reply.

A bitter cry broke from Gracie, and she turned her head away ; but then she remembered the necessity there was for finding out all she could, and, when she looked up, Ralph's miserable appearance moved her to some degree of compassion. After all, *her* grief could not be the same as his, and she said to him, more kindly than ever, " Poor Ralph !" These words melted down all his obstinacy, the hard heart was softened, and he cried bitterly.

" Please, Ralph, tell me all about it," she whispered, coming to his side and seating herself on a rock.

" I will—oh, I will," he sobbed out; "I'm so miserable, I think I shall die."

" How was it ?" said Gracie ; " you came to the rock when I left him, I suppose, and then you laughed at him for not going

with you, and then he said he would, and
then ?"

"Did you see it ?" asked Ralph.

"No; only I think that was the way."

"Yes; and then we were getting eggs:
we clambered down the rocks, and then he
saw a nest and was trying to get them, and
I wanted to get them, and we squabbled
about it, and then I—I pushed him—and
he fell over. I saw him fall; I heard him
scream ; I saw him lying on a ledge of rock
some feet below me; and then I ran away.
I was afraid I should be hung, and so I
would not tell; but I hear him screaming
still. O Gracie, stop him; I think I hear
him even now."

"He may be saved still," said Gracie,
starting to her feet; and then she hurried
home and told all that she knew to her
mother, and they sent off a messenger to
her father at the Point; but the messenger
met him returning, with a face on which
certainty was written instead of suspense;

and as he came near Gracie, he held out a cap which she knew was Frank's.

She quickly told him Ralph's story, and then her father answered,—

" Ay, but for that lad he might have been saved. We searched that ledge of rock, but the tide comes up there at high-water, and he has been washed away. That's his cap; we found it close to the place. My boy is drowned. Both drowned—both dead!" said the wretched man as he entered his cottage; and the mother broke into a wild burst of grief.

Gracie stole away to her little cove, and sat down there. The heavy stupor of tearless grief was over her now; she looked out over the sea, and longed that she was dead too; and then she looked round her little rock-chamber, and saw a hundred things which reminded her of her brother. At last tears came to her relief, and covering her face, she gave way to her sorrow in long piercing cries.

Presently she thought she heard a foot-step, and raising her head, she saw Kenrick standing before her.

"Gracie," he said, more gently than she had ever heard him speak. "Gracie, come with me; I've found something belonging to you."

"Is it anything of Frank?" she said, looking up at him eagerly.

"What's the matter?" said the wrecker, when he saw her tearful face.

"Frank's dead," sobbed Gracie, covering her face again.

"Ay, then those shoes I found did belong to him; come with me and I'll give them to you."

Gracie rose; she did not care where she went, and she followed Kenrick without speaking.

"Were you ever in a place called the Wrecker's Den?" he asked suddenly.

"No," replied Gracie.

"Well, I'll show it to you."

By this time they had reached the Point, and Gracie shuddered as she looked at the rocks; but Kenrick led her on past them till they came to a little sheltered cove, on one side of which some rough steps had been hewn.

"I'll lift you up here," he said; "it's a rough home that I live in, but as I'm leaving it, I don't mind showing it to you!" and then he helped her up the steps, until they came to a large opening in the rock, which was partially concealed by a curtain of creepers which hung down over it. Kenrick pushed them aside, and led Gracie into a large winding cavern. It was very dark, but after going through two or three passages the little girl found herself in a cave of considerable size, into which the light streamed through several fissures in the rock, and which was furnished like a fisherman's hut. In one corner there was a wooden settle, and on this lay a pair of boy's shoes.

Kenrick pointed to them, and Gracie took them up, and stood looking at them very earnestly.

"Well, are they his?" said Kenrick.

"They are," replied Gracie mournfully.

"Then I've got something else of his here, in my sleeping-room," and he led the way into a little inner cave. It was quite dark, but the wrecker found his way to one side of it, and pulling aside another curtain formed of the tangled sea-weed which clung to the outside of the rock, he let the light stream into the cavern, and pointed to a small bed of sea-weed on which lay Frank himself!

He looked very white, but Gracie could hear his regular breathing as he lay there in a sound sleep; and a scream of pleasure broke from her, which made him open his eyes and fix them on her. "Gracie!" he murmured, and then, fancying himself at home, turned round and went asleep again.

"Oh, how did you find him?" she cried, as she clasped Kenrick's hands tightly in

A JOYFUL DISCOVERY.

her own, and looked into his face with thankfulness that could not find words.

"It's a queer story, and it's all your doing, little one."

Gracie looked astonished, and then asked Kenrick to tell her all about it.

"Well, ye see, last night I was in here,

and the tide was coming in, and the waves wash up close to this little cave at the high tide, and all of a sudden I heard a voice underneath me crying—and I didn't care, for I'm a hard man, Gracie; but the tide was coming up faster and faster, and then I heard a wild, loud cry of, ' O mother, O Gracie, I shall never see you again ;' so when I heard your name I pulled aside this sea-weed, and there, on the ledge of rock down below me, lay a boy, whom I knew directly for your little brother Frank; and there was the tide coming up as fast as it could, and the little fellow kneeling down, with his face scared and terrified, and his clothes all torn and jagged; and then there came the remembrance of all your goodness to my little Abel, Gracie, and I determined to run any risk to save your brother; so I fastened a rope securely up here, and I let myself down, and seized his jacket just as the wave was carrying him off, and clambered up again the best way I could."

THE RESCUE.

Gracie's tears were flowing fast, but as Kenrick paused, she looked up and said, " I don't know how to tell you that I thank you."

" I'll tell you, little one ; I'm sick of this life here, and I'm going away to another country far off over the sea—it's what they call emigrating—and, Gracie, you shall think of me sometimes kindly as the man who saved your brother."

" And as Abel's father," said Gracie, softly.

" Yes, child, as Abel's father ; my little boy," he said, with a tender, mournful tone in his voice.

" I wonder how it is Frank isn't more hurt !" said Gracie.

" He's a good deal bruised, but he fell very lightly, and on to a bed of sea-weed instead of the hard rock," said Kenrick.

" Well, I must go and tell daddy and mother," cried Gracie joyfully.

" Wake up, Frank," said Kenrick, bending down over the sleeping boy. " Here's Gracie come to take you home."

"O Gracie, Gracie!" cried the little fellow, springing up. "I was so wicked; I'm so sorry."

"I hope you've learnt a lesson," said Kenrick; and then he added gravely, "if I had minded a father's word, I wouldn't be what I am now. But go, children; look, Frank, there are your boots."

The boy drew them on. "My cap's gone," he said thoughtfully.

"Yes, father brought it home," said Gracie. And then, after many earnest thanks being given to Kenrick, he helped them down the steps, and they went together along the sands.

"Gracie, will father be *very* angry?" said Frank, who was very quiet and subdued.

"I don't think he will," said Gracie; "but, Frank, you'll never disobey him again?"

"I won't; indeed, I won't. O Gracie, when the waves were coming up so close to me, I was so frightened, and I prayed to

God to keep them back; and then when
they kept coming on still, I thought he was
punishing me for being so bad; and I asked
him to forgive me, and to take me to heaven
when I died, for the Saviour's sake; and
then I thought that if he only kept me alive
I would try to serve him all my life."

"FRANK, THERE'S DADDY!"

"Look, look, Frank, there's daddy!" cried
Gracie, and in another instant Frank was in
his father's arms, and all was forgiven.

CHAPTER XII.

FAREWELL TO MOTHER ENGLAND.

"Cheer, boys, cheer! no more of idle sorrow:
  Courage! true hearts shall bear us on our way;
  Hope points before, and shows the bright to-morrow,
  Let us forget the darkness of to-day!"

RACIE slipped away after a little while, and went along the shore to tell Uncle Peter the good news, and on the way she met Ralph, looking more miserable than ever.

"Ralph," she cried, "don't look so sad, don't—he's found—he's at home!"

The boy's whole face lighted up in an instant, and seizing Gracie's arm, he eagerly inquired, "How?"

Gracie, only too glad to find a ready listener, poured out the whole wonderful story. When it was done, Ralph said very earnestly, "I am glad."

"I know you are," said Gracie, "and I am glad for you."

"Will you ever be for forgiving me, or will you hate me always?" asked Ralph in a low voice.

"I have forgiven you long ago," said Gracie. "O Ralph, I wish you would *try* to be a good boy."

"I never could be good in such a home!" said Ralph; and Gracie was inclined to think that he spoke the truth.

"Gracie, you're good, aren't you?"

"No, I'm not."

"I wish I was you."

"Ralph, will you do something for me?"

"Yes, anything."

"Come with me to the Sunday school."

"All right, if I've nothing better to do." And then Gracie went on to Uncle Peter's, and found him as willing to rejoice with her joy as he always was to sorrow with her griefs; and when everything had been told, she returned home, and the evening passed joyfully away.

Jacob had sought out Kenrick and thanked him most cordially, and then made him come back to his house to spend a few hours there in the evening; and Michael Penrose and his wife and baby came too, for Jacob was not content until he had called his friends and neighbours to rejoice with him.

The next evening, Kenrick came to bid Gracie "Good-bye."

"Shall I ever see you again?" asked the little girl.

"No, little one, not here; I'll never come back to England while I live, but I hope to lead a better and honester life in the land I'm going to."

Gracie slipped into the house and whispered something to her mother, and presently she came out with a little Bible in her hand, which she held out to Kenrick, saying, "Please take it; I've got another."

"I will, Gracie, and I'll keep it for your sake. Good-bye, little one;" and wringing her hand, he turned away, and Gracie saw that he was going in the direction of the churchyard to bid farewell to Abel's grave. She never saw Kenrick the wrecker again.

On the following Sunday, she went to call for Ralph to go to the school with them; but when she got to the house, Poll Lennox opened the door and told her to be off with her hypocritical face, for that Ralph had run away to sea.

It was quite true. The boy, weary and wretched in his life at home, had left Hardrick and gone to one of the nearest ports, where he had got a berth as cabin-boy; and his father and aunt felt that they were well rid of him.

CHAPTER XIII.

CONCLUSION.

ONCE more let us glance at the fishers' homes in Hardrick before we close our story. Years have rolled on, and made their changes even in that quiet place. Uncle Peter is laid in his resting-place in the churchyard.

Jacob Williams and his wife are now silver-haired people, and Gracie and Frank are the supports and comfort of their old age.

Simon Lennox has been drowned at sea, and Poll his sister has met at last with the just reward of her evil deeds, and been transported for stealing.

And far away in the backwoods of America there is a lonely grave which covers Kenrick the wrecker; but it is "well with him," for, through the mercy of the Saviour whom Abel had loved, his father has found an everlasting home with his child, where he is waiting to welcome Gracie, who has been like a ministering angel to him.

One evening a sailor had appeared in the village, who seemed very well acquainted with everything concerning the place, and eagerly inquired for the Williams's cottage.

He was not recognized there, for no one would have known the fine manly face and figure of the stranger.

Gracie was sitting with her father at the cottage door, and the sailor held out his hand to her, saying, "Do you remember me, Gracie?"

"No," she replied, looking earnestly at him.

"Well, then, forget that you ever knew me before; forget the sins of my youth. I have grown a wiser and a happier man. I am Ralph Lennox."

RALPH LENNOX'S RETURN.

"Ralph Lennox! Oh, we have so often talked of you, and wanted to hear of you. I am so glad!" said Gracie, holding out her hand to him very cordially, and gazing with extreme pleasure at his honest sunburnt face, so different from that of the obstinate, half-starved boy.

"Yes, Gracie, I have come now to settle down in my native village. I have saved enough money to buy a fishing-boat, and I look forward to a peaceful life in Hardrick, very different from the stormy days of my boyhood."

"Frank," cried Gracie to a tall handsome young man who was coming up the shore with a net in his hand, "here's Ralph Lennox come home!"

And now let us leave the little village of Hardrick while the setting sun is casting its bright beams across the sea. Gracie, we know, will go on steadfastly in the right way, and be a sunbeam to all around her; for "the path of the just is as the shining light which shineth more and more unto the perfect day."

TALES FOR THE HOME CIRCLE.

T. NELSON AND SONS, LONDON, EDINBURGH, AND NEW YORK.

BOOKS OF PRECEPT AND EXAMPLE.

Success in Life. A Book for Young Men. With Plates. Post 8vo. Price 3s.

Seed-Time and Harvest; or, Sow Well and Reap Well. A Book for the Young. By the late Rev. W. K. Tweedie, D.D. Price 2s.

The Boy Makes the Man. A Book of Example and Encouragement for Boys. By the Author of "Records of Noble Lives," &c. With Coloured Frontispiece and Vignette, and numerous Engravings. Royal 18mo. Price 1s. 6d.

Foundation Stones for Young Builders. By the Rev. John Hall, D.D., New York. Royal 8vo. Price 1s. 6d.

Little Things in Daily Life. Little Duties—Little Kindnesses—Little Cares—Little Pleasures, &c., &c. Royal 18mo. Price 1s.

Christian Principle in Little Things. A Book for the Young. With Engravings. Royal 18mo. Price 1s. 6d.

Kind Words Awaken Kind Echoes. Six Engravings. Post 8vo. Price 2s. 6d.

Willing to be Useful; or, Principle and Duty Illustrated in the Story of Edith Allison. With Plates. Post 8vo. Price 2s.

Spare Well, Spend Well; or, Money, Its Use and Abuse. With Coloured Frontispiece. 18mo. Price 1s.

Strive and Thrive; or, Stories for the Example and Encouragement of the Young. Royal 18mo. Price 1s.

Truth is Always Best; or, "A Fault Confessed is Half Redressed." By Mary and Elizabeth Kirby. With Coloured Frontispiece and 17 Engravings. Royal 18mo. Price 1s. 6d.

The Golden Rule; or, Do to Others as You would have Others do to You. Illustrated. Royal 18mo. Price 1s. 6d.

What Shall I be? or, A Boy's Aim in Life. Illustrated. Foolscap 8vo, cloth. Price 2s.

Home Principles in Boyhood, and Other Stories for the Young. Post 8vo, cloth. Price 2s.

Frank Martin; or, The Story of a Country Boy. With Coloured Frontispiece. Foolscap 8vo, cloth. Price 1s. 6d.

Ned's Motto; or, Little by Little. With Coloured Frontispiece, and numerous Engravings. Royal 18mo, cloth. Price 1s. 6d.

Tom Tracy; or, Whose is the Victory? Illustrated. Foolscap 8vo, cloth. Price 1s. 6d.

T. NELSON AND SONS, LONDON, EDINBURGH, AND NEW YORK.

STORY-BOOKS FOR THE YOUNG,

BY THE AUTHOR OF "HOPE ON," &c.

At 1s. 6d. each. Royal 18mo.

The Fisherman's Children; or, The Sunbeam of Hardrick Cove. With Coloured Frontispiece, and 17 Engravings.

Susy's Flowers; or, "Blessed are the Merciful, for they shall obtain Mercy." With Coloured Frontispiece, and 20 Engravings.

Brother Reginald's Golden Secret. A Tale. With Coloured Frontispiece, and 20 Engravings.

King Jack of Haylands. A Tale of School Life. With Coloured Frontispiece, and 18 Engravings.

Little Aggie's Fresh Snowdrops, and what they did in One Day. With Coloured Frontispiece, and 30 Engravings.

The Boy Artist. A Tale. With Coloured Frontispiece, and numerous Engravings.

At 1s. each. Royal 18mo.

Hope On; or, The House that Jack Built. With Coloured Frontispiece. and 25 Engravings.

Martha's Home, and how the Sunshine came into it. With Coloured Frontispiece, and 30 Engravings.

BY THE AUTHOR OF "COPSLEY ANNALS," "VILLAGE MISSIONARIES," &c.

Under the Microscope; or, "Thou shalt call me My Father." With Coloured Frontispiece, and 17 Engravings. Royal 18mo, cloth. Price 1s. 6d.

The Power of Perseverance; or, The Story of Reuben Inch. With Coloured Frontispiece, and 20 Engravings. Royal 18mo, cloth. Price 1s. 6d.

Matty's Hungry Missionary Box, and other Stories. With Coloured Frontispiece, and 30 Engravings. Royal 18mo, cloth. Price 1s.

It's His Way, and other Stories. With Coloured Frontispiece. Royal 18mo, cloth. Price 1s.

The Two Watches, and other Stories. With Coloured Frontispiece. Royal 18mo, cloth. Price 1s.

BY THE AUTHOR OF "THE BABES IN THE BASKET."

The Swedish Twins. Royal 18mo, cloth. Price 1s. 6d.

The Babes in the Basket; or, Daph and her Charge. Illustrated. Royal 18mo, cloth. Price 1s.

T. NELSON AND SONS, LONDON, EDINBURGH, AND NEW YORK.

BOOKS FOR THE LITTLE ONES.

Illustrated Book of Songs for Children. With Music. Edited by the Author of "Hymns from the Land of Luther." Small 4to. With numerous Engravings. Price 3s.

The Illustrated Book of Nursery Rhymes and Songs. With Music. With 37 Engravings by KEELEY HALSWELLE. Small 4to. Price 3s.

Lessons on the Life of Christ for the Little Ones at Home. By the Author of "Hymns from the Land of Luther." With Coloured Frontispiece, and 30 Engravings. Royal 18mo, cloth. Price 1s. 6d.

Little Lily's Travels. With 30 Engravings. Post 8vo, cloth. Price 1s. 6d.

Little Susy's Little Servants. By AUNT SUSAN. Illustrated. Royal 18mo, cloth. Price 1s. 6d.

Little Susy's Six Birthdays. By AUNT SUSAN. Illustrated. Royal 18mo, cloth. Price 1s. 6d.

Little Susy's Six Teachers. By AUNT SUSAN. Illustrated. Royal 18mo, cloth. Price 1s. 6d.

Hymns for Infant Minds, and Original Hymns for Sunday Schools. By ANN and JANE TAYLOR. With Coloured Frontispiece. Royal 18mo. Price 1s. 6d.

Original Poems for Infant Minds. By ANN and JANE TAYLOR. With Coloured Frontispiece. Royal 18mo. Price 1s. 6d.

Johnny; or, How a Little Boy Learned to be Wise and Good. By Mrs. H. C. KNIGHT, Author of "Jane Taylor: Her Life and Writings," &c. With Coloured Frontispiece. Royal 18mo. Price 1s. 6d.

Rhymes for the Nursery. By ANN and JANE TAYLOR. With Coloured Frontispiece. Royal 18mo. Price 1s.

Godliness with Contentment is Great Gain. With Coloured Frontispiece. Royal 18mo. Price 1s.

Happy Little Children: Their Sayings and Doings. By A. S. L. With 17 Engravings. Post 8vo, cloth. Price 1s. 6d.

The Story of a Happy Little Girl. By the Author of "Isabel's Secret." With Frontispiece. Royal 18mo. Price 1s. 6d.

The Cockatoo's Story. By Mrs. GEORGE CUPPLES. With Coloured Frontispiece and 12 Engravings. Royal 18mo. Price 1s.

ELEGANT GIFT BOOKS.
ILLUSTRATED BY GIACOMELLI.
Royal 18mo, cloth extra. Price 1s. 6d.

Songs of Animal Life. Poems by MARY HOWITT. With 90 Engravings.

With the Birds. Poems by MARY HOWITT. With 90 Engravings.

With the Flowers. Poems by MARY HOWITT. With 100 Engravings.

Hymns in Prose for Children. By Mrs. BARBAULD. With 100 Engravings.

T. NELSON AND SONS, LONDON, EDINBURGH, AND NEW YORK.